I0618318

IVAN 2

Her Russian Protector #10

By Roxie Rivera

Night Works Books
3515-B Longmire Drive #103
College Station, Texas 77845
www.roxierivera.com

Publisher's Note: This is a work of fiction. Names, characters, places, and incidents are a product of the author's imagination. Locales and public names are sometimes used for atmospheric purposes. Any resemblance to actual people, living or dead, or to businesses, companies, events, institu-tions, or locales is completely coincidental.

IVAN 2/Roxie Rivera—1st ed.

CHAPTER ONE

*S*TEP. *TOGETHER. STEP. Tap.*

Trying to keep my spine long and my feet nimble, I danced across the gleaming hardwood in the barre studio. We were halfway through our workout, and I was already sweating through my camisole and leggings. The mix of cardio and leg work was killing me.

"And let's add an arabesque!" Mitzi called out from the front of the studio, where she sailed side to side with the ease of a professional dancer.

Step. Together. Step. Lift.

As a little girl in ballet class, this had been one of my favorite movements, and I smiled through the exertion, lifting my arms high as if flying. My thoughts naturally drifted back to childhood recitals, the nervous energy and excitement of flitting across a stage in a poufy tutu and glitter-dusted bun. Memories of Ruby, terrific memories, came back as I mirrored Mitzi's for the next sequence of movement. *Plié. Relevé.*

Ruby and I had been in different dance classes. She had gravitated toward hip hop and jazz while I had been a ballet girl from the first time our mother walked me into the studio at four years old. While I had been a strong dancer, Ruby had been a star. Like every little sister in awe of her bigger sister, I loved to watch and imitate her. Back then, Ruby had welcomed my attention. We had been so close—two sisters who shared everything.

Until the drugs.

"Let's move to first position," Mitzi called out over the music. "And now, sauté!"

Next to me, Zoya leaped like the most graceful Russian ballerina. I shot my friend an annoyed look as she performed every barre movement with the expertise of a dancer who had been classically trained as a child. My jumps weren't nearly as high as hers, probably because I had about seven extra pounds of Christmas cookies and pies weighing me down. I grimaced at my reflection in the classroom mirrors, certain I could see the extra weight jiggling as I landed.

I wanted to blame Vivian for hosting the best Christmas dinner I had ever had, but my willpower was at fault. I had given in to my feelings and crammed two servings of stuffing and sweet potato casserole in my gob before hitting the dessert table and knocking back hot toddies and spiced wine. Two days later, and I was still bloated. Some of it was probably from my period, but most of it was the alcohol and carbs wrecking my digestive system.

When Mitzi directed us to the barre, I pushed loose strands of hair from my forehead and back under my headband. I had decided to let my hair grow out, and it was in that awkward stage where it wasn't quite long enough for a ponytail or bun. Holly kept offering to put in extensions, and I was sorely tempted to schedule an appointment before the Denim and Diamonds fundraising gala on New Year's Eve. *Maybe I should ask Zoya what she thinks.*

"First position," Mitzi announced. "And battement front. Two. Three. Four. Side. Two. Three. Four. And back. Two. Three. Four."

With the pattern of movement explained, I followed along while trying to maintain my form. I tended to tuck my hips in too far and round my back, so I made a conscious effort to keep straight and tall and point my leg correctly. After a few rounds, my thigh was burning from the exertion. I wanted to lower it an inch or two to ease the ache, but Ivan's gruff voice was suddenly in my head, coaching me to keep going the same way he did his fighters.

The image of him standing on the sidelines of a barre class, huge, tattooed arms crossed as he shouted in a mix of Russian and English, made me grin. His high-energy, extremely regimented style of coaching was a complete contrast to Mitzi's friendly, nurturing methods. She enjoyed chatting with us as we wandered into class and slowly eased into the stretching phase. There was no way Ivan would accept his students trickling in and talking. He would be out in the hallway, clapping his massive hands while shouting, "*Davai! Davai! Davai!*"

"What's so funny?" Zoya asked as we switched legs.

"Imagine Ivan as our barre teacher," I panted.

She snorted playfully. "He would have us swinging kettlebells at the barre."

We shared a private giggle and continued to dance. The burn lessened in my standing leg, but it would soon transfer to the other side. I tried to focus on the outcome, of firm but lean legs and a toned and lifted butt. I wasn't ever going to be an athlete like Ivan, but I liked to stay in shape and look good. I also wanted to be healthy when we had a baby.

If we ever have a baby...

The black cloud of infertility hung over me as I followed Mitzi's instructions for the new movement, combining a plié, coupé, and attitude. Because I was still in my mid-twenties, my doctor wouldn't refer me to a specialist until we had tried for more than a year. This last failed cycle had ticked that box, and I had already secured a referral to my chosen clinic.

My cycles came like clockwork, and Ivan was insatiable, so I couldn't understand why it wasn't working. It was hard to see my friends having babies so easily. Benny, Vivian, and Bianca hadn't had any problems getting pregnant. I was so happy for them, and I adored Benny's little girl and couldn't wait for Vivian and Bianca's babies to arrive.

But it hurt. I *hated* feeling that way. The guilt of being so envious was hard to handle. Thank God I could always count on Lena for support. She never judged and always knew exactly what to say. She had even offered to be a surrogate.

Ivan was just as sweet. He didn't put any pressure on me, and I truly believed that he didn't blame me in any way. Obviously, he wanted a baby as badly as I did, but he let me set the pace and make the decisions. He was willing to go as far as I wanted—even IVF—and had made it clear that he didn't want me to even think about the cost. So, I wasn't. I had picked out the best reproductive specialist in Houston.

"Watch your form." Mitzi placed her hand on my back and gave a gentle push to realign my spine. "Keep your chin lifted. Lungs open. Just like that. Good. Very good."

Pulled from my troubling thoughts, I focused on the remainder of the class. When we reached a passé, I made sure to slide my pointed toes along my calf until they rested just above my knee, all while keeping my weight off of my standing leg. After a few grueling seconds of holding the position, we moved from passé into a lunge. The deliberate pace had my thighs shaking and my abdominal muscles screaming by the time we were finished with all the reps on both sides.

When it was finally time to end the session with slow and easy stretches and some yoga, I almost cried out in relief. Flat on my back, I breathed in deeply and then exhaled all the stress of the seemingly endless to-do list that never left my brain. I wanted to stay in the moment. I wanted to enjoy that surge of endorphins from a completed workout and a sense of accomplishment.

"Ladies, what a good class we had today!" Mitzi clapped at the front of the class as we all rose to our feet. Her perky blonde ponytail bounced as she said, "Let's give ourselves a big reverence. We earned it this morning!"

After our graceful bows, the class ended. Zoya tugged her hair elastic from her sagging ponytail and wound her hair into a more tightly coiled bun. "You want to grab some coffee?"

"Sure." I rolled up my yoga mat, tugged on my sneakers, shrugged into the way too big hoodie I had stolen from Ivan's side of the closet, and grabbed my flamingo pink insulated water bottle.

We left the classroom together, stopping at the door to thank Mitzi for another great class. Out in the lobby of the studio, my gaze drifted to the bulletin board and a bright yellow flyer for a new class. I wandered over as Zoya talked to Mitzi about the pilates courses and read the information printed on the flyer.

"Couples yoga?" Zoya read as she joined me at the bulletin board. "If you convince Ivan to go and get a picture, I'll design a special commemorative plaque and frame for the photo evidence."

I laughed and snapped a pic of the flyer for later. "Deal."

"I'd love to design something other than engagement rings and bracelets for mothers," she said as we headed for the double doors. "I lost count of how many last-minute pieces we sold for clients in the run-up to Christmas. On the one hand, it's incredible to know that so many people want to wear my jewelry. On the other hand, I'm exhausted."

"So, take a vacation," I suggested as we stepped out into the cold, rainy morning. I wrinkled my nose at the dreary weather. "Hop a flight to someplace tropical. Enjoy some sunshine and sand while the rest of us deal with this mess."

"I wish, but I can't leave my dad here. He hates beaches," she explained as we walked down the covered walkway of the shopping center. "He also hates taking any time off from the shop."

Knowing how close she was to her father, I decided not to point out that he was a grown man who could handle himself. She and her father had fled Moscow in the middle of the night when she was only a baby after her mother had witnessed a murder and been killed to silence her. From what Ivan had told me, they had barely escaped in time and somehow managed to cross into Estonia before making the journey to Finland and then the US to family in New York.

"Well, maybe take some half days? Go to a spa? Get a massage? Do some self-care?"

She lifted her hand and examined her chipped nail polish.

"I do need a manicure."

"There you go." I reached for the handle of the café we liked. "Schedule some time at Allure. Holly and her staff will take good care of you."

"I do need a trim before the gala," she said, following me into the deliciously scented shop.

"I'm thinking of extensions," I admitted as we stepped into line at the counter. "What do you think? Should I?"

She studied my hair for a moment. "I think you look gorgeous in short hair, and I'm sure you'll look beautiful with longer hair."

"You really are the sweetest," I said, smiling at her.

"Not that sweet," she laughed and cut in front of me to place her order. Before I could whip out my phone to pay, she tapped hers on the card reader and covered my sugary sweet coffee and giant chocolate muffin. As we took seats near the window, she eyed my extraordinarily carb and calorie heavy choices. "Weren't you complaining about your holiday weight gain before class?"

"Well, I mean, yeah, but the holidays aren't over yet, right? We still have New Year's Eve, so it doesn't really make sense for me to start dieting now," I reasoned before taking a huge bite of the decadent muffin.

She snorted with amusement and sipped her blazing hot Americano. "Make sure you dust off all the chocolate crumbs before you get to the Warehouse."

Now, it was my turn to huff with amusement. "Are you kidding me? Ivan knows better than to say anything about what I eat."

"I assume he learned that the hard way?"

"His heart was in the right place, but his brain?" I shook my head. "We agreed that as long as I'm eating a healthy lunch and dinner, what I do for breakfast and snacks is no one's business but my own. And, anyway," I said with a shrug, "his idea of a healthy breakfast is a dozen eggs, a blender pitcher full of some gross protein shake and, like, four gallons of water." I made a face. "No, thanks."

"Gross! Does he really eat a dozen eggs every morning?"

"No, not really," I admitted. "He does a protein shake and tons of water before he goes for his morning run. Then it's four or five eggs plus some salmon or steak and a pile of veggies like kale or tomatoes or sweet potatoes. He has some kind of Greek yogurt and fruit mid-morning. Then he has lunch, his afternoon snack, and dinner."

Zoya's jaw dropped. "How much does it cost to feed him every month?"

"An obscene amount," I muttered and sipped my coffee. "But, every time I growl at him about the grocery bill, he finds ways to distract me."

"Uh-huh," she said knowingly. "I bet he does."

We laughed, but let that topic end there. A busy coffee shop was not the place to discuss those sorts of salacious details.

"So, I heard from a friend that works at a certain PR firm that Ivan's gym is being considered to be the host camp for the next season of that amateur fighting show," Zoya said in a gossipy tone. "True?"

I laughed. "For your friend's sake, I hope Lena doesn't find out someone is blabbing secrets. She'll unleash her dragon lady side."

Zoya smiled. "I never reveal my sources."

"Uh-huh." I sipped my pleasantly warm drink. "True."

"Exciting!"

I shrugged. "It's early in the process. Ivan still isn't sure he'll agree to let them use the gym. He's so protective of the Warehouse and his fighters. Plus," I sighed, "there's that whole, well, *you know*, angle to his life. He doesn't want to bring any attention to it."

"Understandable."

"I hate that choices he made as a kid—like a really young kid—are impacting him now in ways he could never have anticipated back then."

"Life sucks that way," she remarked, not unkindly. "But, people are forgiving and the field he's in doesn't exactly shy away from troublemakers. It might make him even more popular as a coach."

"Maybe." Without much else to say about it, I asked her about the upcoming Denim and Diamonds Gala and the pieces Zoya had donated for the silent auction. She was so modest about the fact her jewelry had been showcased in all of the promo for the event.

"You can downplay it all you want," I said as we sorted our recyclables from trash at the bins by the door, "but Savannah used your jewelry for a reason. She knows it's a draw, and she knows there will be heated bidding over each piece. You should use that to your benefit. Draw in more clients."

"We have a strong client base," she remarked and pushed open the door. "I don't know that I can handle many more commissions."

"Have you and your dad considered expanding? Adding in

more employees on the production side?"

"We talk about it all the time, but he's so hesitant to bring anyone else into our little company. It's frustrating, especially when we're swamped with work, but I understand why he wants it that way. He's protecting what he built, and he's ensuring that it stays something small and intimate. There's a reason we can charge what we do for our pieces."

"That's true." I tugged the hood of my borrowed sweatshirt up over my head as a shield against the cold drizzle and made a face.

As if reading my mind, she said, "At least it's not sleeting."

"Thank goodness," I agreed. "We are not cut out for winter driving around here."

"You should hear my dad when he's driving and there's ice. I'm always afraid he's going to have a stroke yelling at the other cars."

"I can imagine." A memory of Ivan going bananas came to mind. "During the ice storm last winter, Ivan was driving us to dinner, and the shit coming out of his mouth was astounding. I mean, seriously, there were so many Russian swear words flying out of his mouth in combinations I had never imagined. I wanted to take notes, but he forbade it."

She laughed. "I'm sure he did."

Doing my best deep, rumbling impression of my husband, I said, "No, don't ever repeat that! Those words are too nasty for your pretty mouth."

Zoya giggled. "That's a pretty good impression of him."

"My sister's is better," I remarked. "Of course, she's usually doing it to make me mad."

Zoya smiled sympathetically. "When does she get out?"

"A couple of days after New Year's."

"That soon?"

"It's later than we had expected," I explained. "She got into some trouble a few months back, and that meant she had to serve more of her sentence behind bars. She still has a lot of probation, though."

"Do you think she's going to be okay now? Stay clean?"

"I don't know," I admitted reluctantly. "I hope so. I want her to be healthy and happy again. The way she was before the drugs," I added, "but I know that may not be possible. I've been going to these meetings for family members of drug addicts. To prepare for when she comes out," I explained, "and one of the things I've learned is that I need to let go of the idea that she's the same person she was before the drugs. She's been changed by the experiences, and I have to remember that and accept and love this newer, changed version of her."

"I hope for her sake and yours that she's on a better path," Zoya said earnestly. "Will she be going into a halfway house?"

"No, we're letting her stay with us until she gets back onto her feet." My stomach clenched with anxiety. The anticipated friction between my husband and my sister sent my heartbeat into overdrive and that jolt of caffeine I had just had wasn't helping any.

"What's that look for?" she asked as we crossed the parking lot to our vehicles.

"Ivan and Ruby don't get along." Actually, they hated each other, and I hated being in the middle of it.

"Oh no."

"He blames her for all of the trouble she caused and the way she almost got me killed, and she blames him for dragging me into the middle of his connections and getting me kid-napped."

"Yikes."

"Yeah." I opened my purse and started to dig around for my key fob. "Ivan has promised he'll do his best not to respond when she tries to pick fights, and she's promised she won't poke the bear, so to speak."

"How long do you think those promises will last?"

"Ivan has never broken a promise to me, but Ruby has broken so many I've lost count." Annoyed that my post-workout bliss had been crushed by thoughts of my sister and husband at each other's throats, I searched through my purse for my key fob. "But I'm committed to giving her a second chance. I'm going to wipe the slate clean and try to remember that she's starting over after a traumatic experience."

"She may surprise you," Zoya suggested. "She may have changed for good this time. Some people do after hitting rock bottom."

"I hope so." I finally found my keys at the bottom of my too big and overstuffed leather tote. I glanced up to ask Zoya if she wanted to meet for lunch later in the week and immediate-ly noticed the two men in black ski masks striding toward us. "Zoya! Move!"

I snatched her by the arm before she even registered my instruction and jerked her away from the men now running toward us. Still holding onto her arm, I turned to run toward the studio—and slammed right into the chest of a larger man in a similar mask. I froze as the flashbacks of my kidnapping stampeded through my brain. It was just long enough for the other two men to catch up with us.

A man grabbed me from behind, but the grappling lessons Ivan had given me since my kidnapping kicked in on autopilot. I tucked my chin, preventing him from pressing his forearm into my throat, and stepped to the side. He tried to drag me in tighter, but I grabbed onto his wrist with my right hand and scratched down his arm. I balled up my left fist and swung backward as hard as I could, slamming into his groin twice.

"Bitch!" he snarled, leaning forward in pain. I remembered exactly what Ivan had taught me and threw my elbow up into my assailant's face. He cried out in pain and stumbled away from me.

"Zoya!" I yelled her name as I watched her trying to fight off both of her attackers. Feeling emboldened after putting down one man, I launched myself at the attacker on her right, hopping onto his back and punching him in the neck and side of his face. He shouted and tried to fling me off his back, jerking wildly left and right while reaching back to slap at my hands and face. He made one good connection, smacking his knuckles into my cheek just below my eye, and knocked me loose.

With a loud *oof*, I hit the pavement hard. I reached up to touch my throbbing face and felt blood. He had already gone back to trying to drag Zoya away with his friend. Furious that he had managed to hurt me, I scrambled to my feet, snatching up my dropped purse, and swung it with every ounce of power I could muster. It whacked him on the head, and he dropped like a sack of rocks. For once, my overfilled tote had come in handy.

I ran at the man trying to wrestle Zoya to the ground and

kicked him between his legs, hooking the toe of my sneakers into his most vulnerable spot. He made a sound like nothing I had ever heard, a mix of a cry and a scream, and crumpled. Zoya scrambled away from him and toward me.

But my triumphant rush of adrenaline was short-lived.

There was no mistaking the cold bite of steel on the back of my neck. The man I had fought off first had regained his footing and now pressed a gun into my skin with so much pressure I winced. I didn't dare try to escape, not with a loaded pistol that close to my brain.

When he pushed me against the door of my car, I didn't fight him. He pressed his body against mine, thrusting his groin against my bottom in a way that made my stomach lurch. Zoya was shoved next to me, and we exchanged panic glances. The sound of shouting voices from the businesses behind us gave me a burst of hope, but it was quickly snuffed when the third man fired multiple shots into the air.

"Give me your jewelry," the man holding me growled.

With shaking hands, I reached up and unfastened the diamond studs in my ear lobes. I handed them back, and he grabbed my left hand, pushing his knee between my legs to hold me in place. When I realized he was trying to remove my wedding band and engagement ring, I started to fight. "No! Not those!"

He smacked the back of my head, and I jerked forward, whacking my face on the door frame of my car. "I'll take whatever the fuck I want."

With enough force to make me cry out in pain, he wrenched the rings from my left hand and then grabbed my right to pull off the two golden rings I wore stacked on my ring finger there. Ivan had proposed to me with five golden rings, a sweet and romantic play on one of my favorite Christmas carols, and I usually wore at least two of them every day. I said a silent prayer of thanks that I had left two at home that morning.

Placing his mouth close to my ear, my assailant hissed, "You tell your sister to keep her fucking mouth shut or else we'll be back for both of you."

Ruby, what the hell did you do now?

As I tried to make sense of his threat, I shuddered with disgust when he groped my bottom and then slid his hand toward my crotch, running his fingers over parts of me that belonged only to my husband. Knowing how possessive Ivan could be, I jerked my face away and hissed, "My husband will kill you for this."

The man laughed. "He can try."

I was suddenly thrown away from my car, landing on my hands and scraping them. Zoya was tossed next to me. I grabbed for her, dragging her closer and behind me. While one man held his gun on the shopping center behind us, another grabbed our purses and phones. The one who had groped me smashed the windows on my car and then reached into a backpack one of them had brought and produced a pair of bottles with rags stuffed in them. When he pulled a lighter from his pocket, I pushed Zoya back. "Go! Move!"

With a burst of heat and shattering glass, my car caught fire, and the assailants ran from the scene. Dazed by the violent attack, I held tight to Zoya as I watched the car I had worked so hard to pay off became engulfed in a blazing inferno. My worries about bringing Ruby home no longer seemed so important. There was something much, much worse coming for me—and the man I loved.

CHAPTER TWO

ARMS CROSSED, IVAN watched Boychenko try a D'Arce choke from half-guard top. The kid had natural talent, but he seemed distracted this morning. Shaking his head, Ivan stalked across the mat. "No. No. No."

"No? Why?" Boychenko let go of Kir, his grappling partner for the morning, and sat back on his heels.

"Your form is shit." Down on the mat, Ivan motioned for Kir to help demonstrate the proper movements. With his leg locked between Kir's, Ivan slipped his right arm under Kir's left until he could grab the back of his head. He repeated the movement and asked, "See the position of my wrist before I grab the head?"

"Yes."

"You're turning your wrist out and that makes it easy for Kir to escape." Beneath him, Kir relaxed his arm and threw back his head, expertly moving out of the choke. "See?"

Boychenko nodded. "I see."

"When you come in with this right arm, move the left in like this and use both hands to pull his head in toward you." He showed the move twice. "You can't choke in this position, right? You keep lifting this left arm away from Kir, but you have to keep it pressed against his head. See? You run your arm down the back of his head, push it into your chest and then figure four. Just crush the fuck out of him, yeah?"

Kir grunted with discomfort beneath him but didn't tap. Ivan let up a little and said, "Then you drive him back to the mat."

"Why can't I just choke there?"

"Because you aren't big enough," he replied matter-of-factly. "Remember when we talked biomechanics? This is what I meant. Watch."

Kir secured Ivan's leg between his, and Ivan moved in with the submission hold, demonstrating the steps at the regular grappling pace. When he pushed Kir back toward the mat, it took only a second for the other man to tap his arm. Ivan let up immediately and sat back on his heels. "Do you see the difference?"

"Yes."

"Show me," Ivan ordered, staying down on the mat while Boychenko proved he had been paying attention. When the kid had shown a better understanding of the move, he started to show him how to use the choke coming from side mount. He was letting Kir demonstrate on him when Paco, his longtime boxing coach, jogged as fast as his old legs would allow him.

"Vanya!" He waved an iPhone in the air. "I think you need to answer your phone. It's been ringing nonstop on your desk."

Frowning, he moved away from Kir and took his phone from Paco. There were eleven missed calls from numbers he didn't recognize, three from Nikolai and one from Besian. There was a text from the Albanian that said simply, "Call me now!"

He glanced at the time and realized with a sickening thud that Erin was late returning from her barre class. Even if she had gone for her usual after class coffee with Zoya, she should have been back by now, and she always messaged him if she was going to be late. Her lack of contact, the unknown numbers, Nikolai's call, and Besian's message made his heart flip-flop in his chest. He had sudden flashbacks to the night he found out she had been kidnapped and felt a cold panic overwhelm him.

The phone rang again, startling him out of his troubled memories. He answered it gruffly. "Hello?"

"Is this Mr. Markovic?"

He didn't recognize the woman's voice on the other end and started to run toward the office he shared with Erin. "Yes."

"Mr. Markovic, this is Sergeant Levy with HPD. I'm calling to inform you that your wife was involved in a robbery and assault."

His heart stuttered painfully in his chest. He gripped the phone tightly. "Was she hurt?"

"Yes, but not seriously," the sergeant quickly assured him. "She and her friend were taken by ambulance to HCA Houston on Hermann."

"HCA Houston on Hermann," he repeated, grabbing his keys and wallet from his desk drawer. He tried to push the horrible images of Erin bleeding and broken from his mind and focus on what the sergeant was telling him.

"In regards to the car, the fire was put out by HFD. We'll be towing it to the evidence lot for now. An officer is waiting to speak with your wife and her friend at the ER. He can give you the information you'll need for how this situation will progress."

"Yes. That's fine." He slammed his feet into his sneakers and swiped his jacket from the chair where he had tossed it earlier.

"We'll be following up when we get more information from witnesses at the scene…"

He wasn't even paying attention as he rushed from the gym. He reacted like a robot, answering the sergeant when necessary as he dashed out to his SUV. He sped out of the newly resurfaced parking lot, another one of Erin's much-needed changes to the Warehouse, and onto the street, quickly signaling and moving into the turn lane so he could make his way to the hospital.

Guilt soured his stomach as he thought of all the missed calls. How long had they been trying to reach him? Had Erin been asking for him? His gut twisted when he thought of her alone and crying in the back of an ambulance.

What the fuck did not seriously mean? Broken bones? A gashed open head? A black eye? A shattered jaw? He had seen the aftermath of enough fights to know how very little power it took to crunch a human body. Erin had the body of a dancer, petite with curves he had memorized with his hands and mouth, and she was no match for any man in a fight. He had taught her how to defend herself so she could run away, not stand and fight. Had she remembered his lessons? Had she managed to get free?

And why was her car burning? He remembered how proud she was the morning she made her final payment on that car. She had bought it at the beginning of her sophomore year of college and had refused to let him pay it off when they married or upgrade her to something nicer. They had even celebrated receiving the title from the bank with a bottle of her favorite pink champagne. All the hours she had worked at different jobs through college and then later at his gym and doing side gigs as a party planner had gone into that car and her student loans—another thing she refused to let him pay off for her.

Why does this keep happening to her?

She had witnessed so much violence and pain since coming into his life. She had been protected from the worst of it the night his home had been invaded by men trying to find the drugs and money her sister had stolen, but he hadn't been there to protect her the day she had been kidnapped. She had been forced to watch Artyom bleed out on their front steps while men dragged her into a delivery truck.

He could still remember the smell of the old dairy farm where she had been held hostage with Bianca. The memory of her finally safe in his arms was one that never left him. The fear and panic of being told she had been kidnapped always lurked in the back of his mind, often waking him up in the middle of the night.

How many nights had he bolted upright in a cold sweat, terrified he would reach for her and the bed would be empty? How many nights had he been compelled to walk the house, checking windows and doors and the security cameras? He had promised he would take care of her, love her, protect her—but he kept failing.

By the time he found a parking spot in the hospital parking garage, he had all but decided that he was hiring a driver for her. And a bodyguard. Maybe two.

He tamped down his panic as he entered the emergency room and strode toward the registration desk. The woman in front of him was just finishing up so he didn't have to wait long for his turn.

"Can I help you?" the older woman behind the counter asked without even looking up from her computer screen.

"My wife was brought here by ambulance."

"Name?"

"Erin Markovic."

"Her date of birth? Address?" She typed in the information he gave and then directed him to find a chair and wait.

He didn't want to wait. He wanted to see Erin right fuck-ing now, but he pushed aside the urge to demand he be taken to her. The last thing she needed was him making a scene so he took a seat across from the double door entrance to the emergency room.

Almost immediately, he noticed the strange looks and bold stares sent his way. He glanced down at his shorts and bare legs and grimaced. He tried to keep the evidence of his criminal past covered in public, but he had been in such a rush to get here it had been the last thing on his mind. There were only a few centimeters of skin from his toenails to his neck that weren't tattooed, and everything was on display to anyone curious enough to look.

The double doors opened and nurse called, "Mr. Mar-kovic?"

He stood quickly and joined her at the door. There was no mistaking the way her soft smile hardened as she took in his tattooed hands and legs. It didn't bother him, but he hated knowing that Erin would be treated differently once people realized she was married to a criminal.

Former criminal, he silently corrected as he followed the nurse into the emergency room.

Wordlessly, the nurse tugged aside a curtain to reveal Erin sitting in a hospital bed looking impossibly small and vulnerable. She had one of his old hoodies draped across her legs, A small cut on her cheek had been closed with strips and another on her temple had been closed the same way, but the gash on her hairline had been sutured. There was dried blood on her chin and neck and under her nose. Her upper lip was swollen and the tiny straps of her workout top made it easy to see the angry red bruises on her upper arms and shoulders.

Rage burned through him. Some piece of shit had dared to put hands on her. He swore then that he would find that asshole and make him pay.

"Ivan!"

Her tears and the way she said his name were like a knife to the chest. Rushing toward her, he carefully cupped the back of her neck and kissed her forehead and then both cheeks. "I'm here, baby. I'm here." He wrapped his arms around her and held tight. "What happened?"

"They came out of nowhere!" She clung to his jacket and burrowed into him. "I saw the first two guys behind Zoya and then there was another guy behind me. I tried to fight them off. I remembered what you taught me and got away from him, but then we started fighting and the other one threw me on the ground. They stole my rings and burned my car," she babbled between sobs.

Ivan's mind reeled as Erin unloaded her panicked

thoughts on him. He glanced at her hands and noticed the raw skin where her rings had been forcefully yanked off her fingers. The idea that some asshole had stolen her engagement and wedding rings angered him. The thought that they would be fenced and melted down sickened him.

"He said that if Ruby doesn't keep her mouth shut they'll be back." She sobbed harshly. "And then he touched me," she wept, pressing her face into his chest. "He put his hand between my legs, and he…he…" She sobbed loudly, unable to continue her description of the assault. "I told him you would kill him for touching me like that."

I will. Slowly. Painfully.

Fucking Ruby. That girl was a goddamn menace. He didn't even want to imagine what kind of bullshit she had gotten tangled up in while doing her time. Couldn't she go one single fucking year without putting Erin in danger?

He shoved down the fury that threatened to erupt and focused only on Erin. She didn't need the mean, savage side of him right now. She needed comfort and love and the protection and security of his arms around her. Drawing her in closer, he nuzzled her ear and neck. He would do anything to make her stop crying. It was tearing out his fucking heart to hear it and to know she had been so scared and so hurt.

He shifted onto the uncomfortable hospital bed and dragged her onto his lap, draping her legs sideways across his thighs. He cradled her closely, tugging the hoodie she had borrowed from his closet over her legs to keep her warm. As he gently stroked her back, she nestled in, sliding her arms around his neck and crying softly.

He couldn't stop the painful thoughts racing through his

mind. Having been abandoned as a child, he had always been plagued with the very real belief that he wasn't good enough for anyone to love. He had always believed something inside him was rotten and unlovable. He had considered himself unworthy of a wife and family.

Until Erin.

She loved him unconditionally. From the first moment she stepped into his life, she had accepted him and his faults and his murky past. She had soothed that raw, festering wound deep inside him and helped him believe that he was worthy of all the things he had always wanted.

Yet he couldn't shake the feeling that he had ruined her life. He had dragged her into the seedy underbelly he could never escape, and now she was suffering the consequences of associating with him.

As if the universe wanted to kick him square in the balls and make him feel even worse, the curtain closing off her emergency room cubicle shifted aside and none other than Detective Eric Santos stepped into the space. Ivan silently cursed the arrival of the nosy detective. The last thing Erin needed was to be questioned relentlessly by someone who hated him and the crime family he had once served.

"Erin," Detective Santos greeted with a nod. He glanced briefly in Ivan's direction. "Ivan."

Ivan had never wanted to be on a first name basis with a cop, but here they were. "Detective," he said with a grunt of annoyance.

"I know you're about to be discharged, but I wanted to ask you a few questions before you leave," Detective Santos explained. "Is that okay?"

Erin nodded. "Sure."

Eric's gaze shifted to Ivan who still held his wife across his lap. "I want to speak with her alone."

Ivan started to protest, but Erin touched his jaw. She held his gaze, silently communicating with him in the way that husbands and wives often did. He understood and nodded stiffly before moving her off his lap and onto the bed. He tenderly kissed her. "I'll be right outside if you need me."

On his way out of the room, he fixed the detective with a warning glare. He closed the curtain behind him and leaned against the wall, arms crossed as he listened to whatever Santos had to say to his wife.

"Why are you here?" Erin asked testily. "I've already spoken to the officers who responded and to the other robbery detective who came to see me. I thought you were in guns and gangs or something like that."

"I am," Santos confirmed. "I suspect this robbery and assault may have ties to a gang. Or," he added, "that it may be connected to your husband's ties to a certain criminal organization."

"My husband owns and operates an elite MMA training camp and gym, Detective Santos. There's nothing criminal about our business."

"If you say so," Santos replied in that rude fucking way of his. "I've already spoken to your friend, Zoya. She didn't have anything to add to her statement she gave police at the scene, but she did mention that one of the men seemed to be talking to you when he had you pressed up against your car. Can you tell me what he said?"

"I'd rather not."

"Why?"

"Because."

"Because you're trying to protect your husband? Or maybe your friends and their husbands?"

"No," Erin snapped. "I'd rather not relive the moment when a disgusting stranger put his hand between my legs and told me what he was going to do to me."

Santos was silent for a long moment. "I'm sorry, Erin. I didn't know about that part of the assault. It wasn't in the report I got from the officers on the scene."

"Well, now you know." She sighed loudly. "Listen, there's nothing sinister or nefarious happening here. Okay? It was just a robbery. I was in the wrong place at the wrong time."

"If it was just a robbery, why did they burn your car?"

"Probably because they had their hands all over it? They wanted to destroy evidence. I don't know. I'm not a criminal. I don't have any answers for their behavior."

"Bullshit," Santos protested. "I think you're lying to me, Erin. I think something else happened in that parking lot. Whatever you're hiding—whoever you're trying to protect— I'll figure it out. I can promise you that. When you're ready to talk, to be honest with me, you know where to find me."

The curtain jerked open as Ivan shoved off the wall, ready to give Eric a piece of his mind. The detective turned back toward Erin and said, "Tell your sister I said, 'Hi.' I'm sure I'll be seeing her again soon. From what I've heard about her time in jail, she's one stumble away from picking up that nasty habit of hers."

"Fuck. You." Erin glared at the detective. "You come near my sister or try to harass her in any way, and I'll make your life a living hell."

Santos laughed. "I'm sure you'll try."

Ivan clenched his fists at his sides. He wanted nothing more than to slam his fist into Eric's smug face, but he wrestled the urge down and simply stared down the detective until he pivoted on his heel and left. The last thing he needed was to catch a charge for knocking out a detective. Once Eric was gone, Ivan stepped into the room and closed the curtain. Erin held out her hand, and he took it. "I'm sorry, *angel moy*."

"Don't apologize for him. He's such a dick."

"He is, but he's taking out his frustration with me on you. That's not right."

"No, it's not, but it is what it is." She placed her hands on his waist and tugged him closer. She placed her cheek against his chest and ran her fingers up and down his lower spine. "Please don't ask me to put Ruby on the streets instead of in our house when she gets released."

Taken aback, he said, "I wouldn't ask you to do that."

"I know how much you two dislike each other," she replied, soothing him with her stroking fingers.

Dislike was a tame word for what he felt for her older sister. Still, he said, "You let Ten stay with us even after they raided the house and tossed his room."

"I was pretty upset," she reminded him. "It's hypocritical of me to ask you not to refuse to let Ruby stay with us."

"You're her sister. You're family." He tilted her chin up and gazed down into her beautiful eyes. "*We're* family."

She smiled up at him, her expression soft and loving. "Thank you."

He brushed his thumb along her cheek. Even though it

aggravated him that yet again they had to clean up one of Ruby's messes, he said, "Because we're family, I'll find out what trouble she's in and handle it if I can."

"Ivan, you don't need to do that. You've already done so much for her and for me."

"You're my wife, Erin." He traced her lower lip with his thumb, letting it linger on the swollen edge and feeling another flare of anger that someone had dared to touch her. "I'll do whatever is necessary to keep you safe. I swore to you after the kidnapping this shit would never happen again—but here we are."

"This isn't your fault."

"It is."

"How?"

"If I was still *in*, no one would ever think to come after you."

"If you were still *in*," she emphasized to let him know that she understood that he meant the mafia, "we wouldn't be together. You would have never have let me get close to you."

She was right. He wouldn't have. He would have helped her with Ruby and then sent her on her way. He would have watched after her from afar and fantasized about what sort of life he might have with a girl like her.

"Maybe it's a scam," she offered, dragging him away from those maudlin thoughts. "Maybe what happened today is someone trying to set up a blackmail type scenario to get money out of us."

"Do you think your sister would be in on something like that?" He thought Ruby absolutely would try to fuck him that way, but he wasn't sure that she would have allowed someone to hurt Erin like this. Throughout her time in jail, Ruby had shown actual remorse for the way she had put Erin in danger.

"No," Erin answered immediately. "Whatever her faults—and she has a lot—she would never do something like this for money. She would come straight out and ask."

"It's no secret that she's related to us," he reasoned. "If someone she met on the inside thinks they can use her connection to us to get money, they might try it. People do crazy shit for cash."

"That's true," she agreed. A moment later, she said, "Or…"

"Or?" He pulled back so he could look down at her. "What are you thinking?"

"What if someone is trying to drive a wedge between us? What if someone wants to poison us against Ruby? Or turn me against you by using my sister? Maybe something really bad is coming, and they want us vulnerable."

He started to dismiss her worries, but experience made him reconsider. His past was murky and dark, filled with terrible misdeeds and crimes. Ruby's past wasn't quite as bad as his, but she had pissed off a lot of people in the Houston underworld. There was no shortage of bad characters who wanted to hurt him or Ruby. Hurting Erin was the easiest way to accomplish that.

Erin's small hand touched his jaw, drawing his attention back to her. She smiled up at him. "Take me home?"

Nodding, he lowered his head and claimed her mouth in a gentle kiss. Once he had her safely at home, he would start calling in favors and markers until he got the names of the assholes who had hurt her. After that—all bets were off.

CHAPTER THREE

"I'M FINE!" I protested as Vivian fussed around me, tucking a blanket around my waist after handing me a cup of my favorite cinnamon spice tea. She had arrived on my doorstep almost as soon as we had and immediately started mothering me. If ever there was a woman born to nurture, it was Vivian. "If anyone needs to rest, it's you."

She followed my gaze to her baby bump. "I'm getting so much rest I'm going stir crazy. Nikolai has been impossible the last few days."

"He just wants everything to be perfect," Lena piped up from her spot by the fire. She had taken a very fussy Sophia from a harried Benny and played with her on the fluffy white rug there. "With everything that's happened this year, our guys are on edge." She made a silly face at Sophia who giggled gleefully and made silly baby sounds. "Yuri barely lets me out of his sight when we're here. I have more freedom to roam when we're back in Russia."

"Dimitri added more cameras to our house." Benny enjoyed her cup of tea while kicked back on the chair closest to her daughter. "He put in more at the bakery, too. He basically has eyes on me and Sophia day and night."

"Sounds like the plot to a psycho husband thriller on *Life-*

time," Lena remarked.

"I think it sounds like a loving father and husband doing his best to keep his family safe," Vivian insisted before shooting Lena an annoyed look.

"It was weird, at first," Benny admitted, "but there are apps on our phones that let us check in during the day. If I'm at the bakery, I can open the app and see the two of them having breakfast or playing. If he's late coming home, he can check all the doors and windows and drop in on the nursery to watch our bedtime routine."

"See?" Vivian's brows arched as she pinned Lena in place. "Dimitri is a good dad and husband."

Lena made a rude face at Vivian, causing Sophia to giggle. Distracted by the baby, she said, "Is Ivan going to allow your sister to come here when she gets out of jail?"

Remembering the shocked look on his face when I had asked that question earlier in the emergency room, I nodded. "We talked about it, and we've agreed she's still coming here."

"I think you're making a mistake." Lena gently tugged her hair from Sophia's hand and gave her the chunky wooden bracelet from her wrist. "It's a risk to let her back into your life."

"She's family," Vivian argued. "We don't turn our backs on family. If we did, all of us would be alone right now. All of us have had issues with our siblings or parents. None of us are perfect. Ruby made a mistake. She went to jail. She served her time. She deserves a chance to prove herself."

"My brother turned his life around," Benny interjected. "If she has the right support system, Ruby can make a change for the better."

"Sure," Lena agreed, "but Erin got attacked today because of something her sister did or knows. That's not going to go away just because Ruby gets her life together."

"And that's what our men are discussing right now," Vivian stated rather imperiously. "They'll figure out the best way to handle it." She tucked her skirt around her knees in a prim gesture. "Now," she said in a tone that signaled the end of that line of discussion, "what are we going to do about Erin's bruises and sutures? She can't walk into Denim and Diamonds looking like she tussled in a cage match."

Grateful for Vivian redirecting our discussion away from Ruby, I said, "I've been thinking about getting extensions. Maybe if one of the stylist's at Allure can work me in, I can get them done before the gala."

"You can have my appointment tomorrow afternoon with Nisha," Lena offered. "I can hold off on my cut and color until her next opening."

"Are you sure?" I knew how hard it was to get on Nisha's book, and Lena had been going to her for years.

"Totally fine," she said with a wave of her hand. "I'll give her a call. If it's okay with her, the appointment is yours."

"Thank you."

"Here." Lena stood up and thrust Sophia at me. "You're on baby duty while I make that call."

Sophia happily clambered onto my lap, standing on my thighs to examine my face. Her big eyes took in my bruises, and she seemed to decide that pulling my hair or poking at me wasn't the best idea. Instead, she wiggled around and plopped down on my lap, blowing raspberries and kicking her little feet. Her soft hair smelled of citrus and vanilla as I gently brushed my fingers through the wavy curls. After all the playful roughhousing with Lena, Sophia was sleepy and turned to cuddle against me. Enjoying every moment of baby snuggles, I listened as Vivian and Benny talked about their outfits for the gala.

My thoughts drifted toward Ivan and the men in his office. Whatever they were discussing, he would try to keep it from me. He always tried to shield me from that side of his life, and after the kidnapping that had happened right here on our front steps, he was paranoid about keeping me safe. Considering what had happened today, he would probably be consumed with worry.

My gaze drifted from the sweet armful of snuggly baby cuddled up against me to the entryway of the house. I tried not to think about the day Artyom had been shot and I had been taken. The memories made me feel panicked and anxious. They made me feel uncomfortable and nervous in our home.

That first day back in our home after the kidnapping, I had immediately wanted to sell. I wanted out of here. I wanted a new start in a new place without any bad memories, but I hadn't been able to work up the courage to tell Ivan how I felt. I didn't want to heap anymore guilt on his shoulders, and I wasn't sure he would understand why I wanted to go somewhere else.

He was the sort of person who always faced his fears. He wasn't afraid to take on any enemy or threatening situation. I suspected his extremely difficult childhood had made him so brave and resolute. It was one of the things I loved most about him. He was utterly steadfast and true. There was nothing and no one he wouldn't fight for me.

Except I didn't want him to have to fight anyone ever again. Just as he wanted to keep me safe, I wanted the same for him. I wanted him to leave that part of his life where it belonged: in the past. If he went looking for trouble, he would find it—and then what? What would happen to the life we were building together? To our marriage? Our business? The children we wanted?

I couldn't live with one foot in both worlds the way Vivian did. She seemed to have been born to be a mafia don's wife. She moved elegantly and easily through her life as a wealthy businessman's wife one minute and a ruthless mob boss's woman the next. She kept a beautiful home, painted incredible works and loved her husband with the sort of fierceness that could be terrifying. There was a steely hardness to her that other people didn't see. Nikolai might be the one who was known for his merciless control of the underworld, but it was Vivian who posed the greatest danger to anyone who threatened her family.

"Nisha is going to see us both at the same time," Lena said as she slid onto the sofa in the space next to me. "She has a new girl she's training who is going to take most of my appointment. She worked on my hair the last time I was in Nisha's chair so I'm comfortable with it."

"Thank you, Lena. I really appreciate it."

"It's the least I can do." She reached out to swipe a beautifully manicured finger down Sophia's chubby little cheek. "I think I might actually want to have more than one of these."

I snorted softly. "You can't even say the word baby?"

"I don't want to jinx myself." She held Sophia's hand and seemed to marvel at her tiny fingers. "I'd rather not walk down the aisle with a beach ball belly."

"You'd still be a beautiful bride."

"But I wouldn't fit into the dress I picked, and it's *the* dress."

The whirlwind trip to New York City to find that couture gown had been some of the most fun I had had in ages. Yuri had splashed out on the best of everything, putting us up in a penthouse with an incredible view of Central Park and arranging the hardest to get tickets to Broadway shows and reservations at the hottest restaurants. I shuddered to think what it must have cost him to send the five of us girls all that way. The price tag on the gown was scary enough!

"What about your…?" Her gaze lowered to my flat belly. "Any progress?"

I shook my head. "Aunt Flo is in town."

"I'm sorry," she said softly and gave my hand a squeeze. "My offer still stands."

A few months earlier, she had offered to be a surrogate if the issue keeping us from getting pregnant was something to do with my womb. It wasn't an offer she made lightly, and I had no doubt that if I came to her and asked her to carry a baby for me, she would drop everything to make it happen. It was times like this that she proved what a big, selfless heart she had.

"Benny just had a great idea," Vivian announced. "We should all meet up for brunch the morning after the gala."

"Not at Samovar," Lena said, wrinkling her nose.

"Why not?" Vivian bristled.

"We *always* eat at your restaurant."

"No, we don't," Vivian argued.

Lena dramatically rolled her eyes and started to list off all the times we had met at Nikolai's famed restaurant for shared meals. As the two bickered back and forth, I shared an amused smile with Benny and let my thoughts turn back to Ivan and the meeting in his office. *What the hell are they talking about in there?*

CHAPTER FOUR

WORRIED THAT ERIN might be overwhelmed by all of the people who had descended on their house, Ivan glanced at his watch for the second time in the last ten minutes and wondered how quickly he could run everyone off without being a rude asshole.

"Did she manage to get a good look at them?" Dimitri asked, pulling Ivan from his thoughts.

"They were in all black. Masks. Shirts. Pants. Boots. She thinks they were all white men. Two of them had green eyes. She remembers that very clearly. They were fit and shorter than me. That's all I got out of her."

"It probably happened so fast that she didn't have time for details," Dimitri reasoned. "It's a good thing you were teaching her self-defense."

"I shouldn't have to teach her how to fight," he growled, hating that his wife was forced to brawl in the fucking street to defend herself. "She should be able to walk to her car without getting attacked."

"Yes, she should," Dimitri agreed, "but the world is a fucked up and dangerous place. You gave her the skills she needed to protect herself. You should be proud of her for not freezing."

"I am proud of her." He didn't even have the right word to describe how proud he was of his wife.

"What do you think they meant?" Yuri asked as he helped himself to a splash of Canadian whiskey. "Keep her mouth shut about what?"

"Fuck if I know," Ivan replied, slashing his hand through the air when Yuri gestured toward him with the bottle. He wasn't in the mood for a drink right now.

"It has to be something that Ruby saw in jail," Nikolai reasoned. "We made sure all of Ruby's debts and other problems were handled before you married Erin. There's nothing else out there."

"She may have seen something in one of the drug dens she used to visit," Dimitri suggested. "She may have seen a murder or some other crime?"

"Maybe," Ivan said uncertainly. He caught Nikolai's gaze. Both men had spent time in prisons back home, and both understood more than Yuri or Dimitri ever would about the sort of horrible shit that happened behind bars. "I worry she saw something happen in jail."

"Like inmate on inmate?" Yuri took a seat and sipped his whiskey. "Or something worse? The guards doing something they shouldn't?"

"If that's the case, we're going to have a hell of a time finding out what it was," Dimitri remarked.

"When is Kostya back?" Yuri asked. "This is what he does best."

"He almost died," Dimitri said with irritation. "His heart actually stopped. You're really going to sit there and ask when he's coming back from Mexico to start chasing down dangerous leads?"

"It's his job," Yuri replied matter-of-factly.

"Was," Nikolai interrupted. "It was his job."

"And what exactly does a retired cleaner do?" Yuri wondered. "Do you really think he's just going to stop being what he is? A fixer? A spy? An assassin?" Yuri shook his head. "He'll come back when he's ready, and he'll want to do what he does best."

"Not for me," Nikolai stated. "He can freelance if he wants, but his days of cleaning up our shit are over."

"You better find a new housekeeper then," Yuri advised. "The underworld is a dirty, messy place. You don't want to track all that muck back to your clean, tidy house."

"I don't need you to tell me how things are, Yuri." Nikolai's eyes hardened in a way that would have made lesser men avert their gazes and apologize. Not Yuri, though. He had been pushing Nikolai's buttons since they were children. Clearly not wanting to argue, Nikolai ended that line of discussion with a simple, "It's all being handled."

"I may have a way to get some information about the jail," Dimitri said, his gaze focused on his phone. "One of our guys is married to a woman who used to work there as a detention officer. I'll see if she's willing to talk to me about her experience there. She might know something useful." He slipped his phone back into the pocket of his jeans. "I'll be vague. Careful," he added. "Until we know more, I don't want to raise any suspicions."

"What about our detective friend?" Yuri asked, his expression grim and irritated as he mentioned Eric.

"He was at the hospital." Ivan held Nikolai's gaze, noticing the slight narrowing of Nikolai's eyes.

"What did he want?" Dimitri looked worried. "He doesn't work robberies."

"He thinks Erin and Zoya are lying and hiding the real reason for the attack. He thinks it's something to do with my past."

"That's all we need," Yuri grumbled. "Eric fucking Santos digging through our lives again. If he goes after Ruby…"

He let the thought hang unfinished. It was no secret to anyone in the room that Ruby was the weak link.

"There's nothing to worry about there," Nikolai decided. "She's nothing to me or any of my soldiers and captains. Whatever she thinks she knows is complete and total bullshit. If she spins a tale for Eric, let him waste time chasing it down."

"What about Zoya?" Yuri relentlessly prodded, bringing up yet another complication.

"She knows more about keeping quiet than most of us," Nikolai remarked. He didn't have to say anything more than that. They all knew the terrible story of Zoya's mother.

"Other than chasing down some leads, what else can we do to help, Vanya?" Dimitri asked. "Do you want me to send some of my men to guard Erin? Have them tail her if you'd rather keep it low-key?"

He rubbed his face and admitted, "Erin will lose her shit if I hire a bodyguard without asking her. I wanted to call you at the hospital and hire someone right then and there, but I didn't want to upset her."

"Talk to her," Dimitri urged. "If she's agreeable, we can find someone she likes."

"I will." He already knew what her answer would be. "The

most important thing to her is getting back her rings."

Dimitri winced. "I doubt that's possible."

"I know," he agreed, "but I have to try. I've already spoken to Besian. He used his pawn shop connection to get the word out that I want them back. If someone tries to get rid of them at a pawn or gold shop in town, I'll find out about it."

"If those assholes are smart, they'll melt them down or throw them away," Yuri warned.

"If they were smart, they wouldn't have attacked the wife of one of my best friends." Nikolai glanced at his watch. "Speaking of wives, I need to get mine home."

Dimitri followed Nikolai's example and stood. "It's time for my girls to have their afternoon nap."

"I thought Benny had taken a break from opening the bakery?" Yuri asked before polishing off the whiskey in his glass.

"There was a family emergency with one of her longtime employees," Dimitri explained. "She's back on early mornings until Connie's mom is out of the stroke unit and into a rehab center." He made a face. "But, fuck, that alarm at three in the morning is rough."

"She needs to delegate to another employee," Yuri advised, taking his dirty glass in one hand and slapping Dimitri on the back with the other. "I get it. She's proud of her business. She's protective of what her family built, but she deserves to enjoy the perks of being the owner…"

Ivan watched Dimitri and Yuri leave the office. Nikolai had remained behind, clearly hoping to catch him in a private moment. Worried he wouldn't like whatever the boss had to say, he sighed and asked, "What?"

"Despite what I said earlier, if this girl is going to be a problem, I expect you to handle it."

Ivan blew out a noisy breath. "You're talking about my wife's sister."

Nikolai's eyes were stone cold. "I know exactly what I'm saying."

Ivan gritted his teeth and didn't argue. He nodded stiffly. "I'll handle it."

"I know you will." Signaling that he was finished discussing it, Nikolai rose and buttoned the front of jacket.

Fighting the urge to give Nikolai the finger for being so highhanded, he followed him back into the living room where their wives had congregated. He found Erin sitting in the corner of her favorite couch with little Sophia tucked in her arms. Their gazes met, and his earlier irritation with Nikolai fled. Seeing her with Dimitri's little girl filled him with a longing he couldn't quite articulate. The idea that someday soon Erin would hold their baby, their son or daughter, made his heart do a funny little flip in his chest.

After sharing private, tender smiles, he herded everyone out the door in groups of two and three until only Vivian and Nikolai remained. She had disappeared into the kitchen and emerged a short time later. As Nikolai helped her into her coat, she said, "I put lunch in the oven. Take off the foil when the timer goes off and give it another twenty minutes or so. There's a salad and dessert in the refrigerator. Lena left a bottle of wine on the counter."

"Thank you." Erin hugged Vivian.

"Call me later."

"I will."

"Vanya." Nikolai nodded, silently communicating that he would be a phone call away if they needed anything.

He followed the couple to the front door and locked up behind them, checking the security system before returning to the living room. Erin had moved to the loveseat closer to the fire. He crouched down to add another log and rearrange the glowing coals. When the fire was burning hot the way she liked, he joined her on the loveseat, sinking into the deep, plush cushions and opening his arms. She cuddled into his embrace, placing her head against his chest and wiggling in closer. He held her tightly, knowing that she needed to feel safe.

As he combed his fingers through her hair, he said, "When Ruby calls you, don't say anything about what happened today."

She didn't seem surprised by his request. "I wasn't planning to," she replied. "I…I want to see her face when she finds out. It's the only way I'll know if she's…well…you know."

"I know." He understood her reticence. She didn't want to accuse her sister of setting her up, especially when it was likely that Ruby was a victim of something terrible.

"What do you think they want her to be quiet about?" Erin asked, her voice filled with worry. "Like…a murder?"

He winced at the possibility. "Fuck, I hope not."

"Drugs? Maybe some kind of dealing inside the jail?"

"Probably." He didn't want to tell Erin that he feared it might be something worse than drugs. Jails and prisons here were different than the ones back home, but they weren't *that* different. There was a fair chance that some kind of forced prostitution or sexual coercion was going on behind the walls of the jail. The type of men who wanted to be guards seemed to have an affinity for playing power games with inmates. He had seen it plenty of times during his short stints as a teenager and then young adult. Whatever went on in women's jails had to be a hundred times worse than what went on in the men's side.

"I'm getting my hair done with Lena tomorrow."

Her comment pulled him away from those old, horrible memories. "Yeah?"

"I'm getting extensions."

In all the time they had been together, he hadn't ever seen her with long hair. It would be a novelty to see her look so different so quickly.

Misreading his silence, she glanced up at him with doubt in her eyes. "Is that okay?"

"Erin." He tipped her chin and claimed her mouth. Holding her gaze so she would know he meant it, he said, "You could shave your head tomorrow, and you would still be the most beautiful fucking woman I've ever seen." With a grin, he added, "I would miss being able to pull your hair when we're in bed, but I'm sure I could find something else that would make you scream."

She snorted playfully and pressed a noisy kiss to his jaw. "Wow. So romantic!"

"Make sure to ask them to put those extensions in extra tight," he teased. "If you want them to last longer than one night."

"Ivan!" Laughing, she swatted at him. "Stop!"

"Not a chance," he murmured against her mouth, careful of her bruised bottom lip. When he dragged her onto his lap, hauling her thighs over his until she straddled him, she sighed happily and rocked against him. Not wanting to push her into being intimate after what she had experienced that morning, he asked, "Do you still want me to stop?"

"Nope." She gripped the back of his neck as he kissed his way down her neck to the curve of her shoulder peeking out of her oversized sweater. "But—."

"But?"

"I'm on my period."

"Like that's ever stopped me before," he muttered and nipped at her skin. "Are you using *it*?"

Before Erin, he had never given much thought to women's cycles or the ways they handled them. Once she had moved in with him, he had become quickly acquainted with things like cups and discs and all of the interesting benefits they had—including allowing them to be intimate anytime they wanted.

"Yes," she whispered, her voice shaky as he traced his fingers along the seam of her leggings, right between her plump cheeks.

"Good."

Her short nails bit into the back of his neck as he slipped his hand into her leggings. Exhaling with need, she begged, "Make me forget how gross that other guy made me feel when he touched me. Take me upstairs and fuck me. Remind me that I belong to you—and only you."

"Fucking right you do," he growled and captured her mouth. Overcome with the need to claim her, to mark her like a wild beast would its mate, he thrust his tongue against hers. As he stood holding his wife in his arms, her thighs wrapped around his waist, the animalistic side of him entertained violent thoughts of retribution and revenge against that piece of shit who had assaulted her.

Mine. She's mine. And I'll kill the next man who dares to touch her.

Carrying her upstairs to their bedroom, he silently vowed that the men who hurt her would regret the day they decided to threaten his family. They had no idea what was coming for them.

CHAPTER FIVE

S TEPPING CLOSER TO the full-length mirror in the corner of our walk-in closet, I studied my appearance. The bruises from my ordeal outside the barre studio had faded enough that careful application of color correcting concealer made them disappear under my foundation. I had gone a little heavier with my eyeshadow and liner to draw attention away from the areas I had camouflaged.

Sweeping aside my freshly cut bangs, I reluctantly admitted to myself that Lena and Nisha's insistence that I needed them was correct. They framed my face and highlighted the shape of my eyes and my cheekbones. I finger combed the waves of luscious brown hair tumbling around my shoulders, some of it mine and some of it extensions, and marveled at how different I looked. Nisha's prices were exorbitant, but she was worth every single penny.

"Do I have to wear this?"

I stepped into my heels and left the walk-in closet to find Ivan decked out in his tux and standing in front of the mirror, tugging at his bolo tie. I gently swatted his hands away. "Stop. It took forever for me to tie this just right."

"I look ridiculous," he groused, eyeing his reflection with distaste.

"You look sexy." I spread my hands across his broad chest, feeling the starched white fabric of his dress shirt before sliding my hands up and over the crisp black tuxedo jacket. "The dress code is non-negotiable for Denim and Diamonds."

"I look like an extra in *Urban Cowboy*!"

Regretting our 80's movie night, I sassily replied, "Well, smack my butt and call me Sissy because I'm about to climb you like a mechanical bull."

He made that growling sound that made my insides wobble before slapping my bottom with one of his big hands. I yelped, and he swallowed my cry of protest with one of his punishing kisses, making me ever so grateful I had used a smudge proof color tonight. When he pulled back, he said, "You can climb on me anytime."

"Later."

"We can be late."

"No." Even though my body was on fire and screaming yes, I declined his tempting offer for a bathroom quickie. "This is our first year going, and I want to make a good impression."

He frowned. "Why? Who cares what these people think?"

"I care." I gently adjusted the collar of his shirt. "Our business is growing. The properties you own—"

"*We* own," he corrected, reminding me that he insisted everything he owned before we got married was mine once I shared his last name.

"The properties *we* own are going up in value, and a few of them are along the new I-45 expansion. We're going to want to diversify like we talked about a few weeks ago. We need connections to people outside of our group of friends. If we want to reach all those goals we discussed, this is part of it. We have to schmooze."

"You schmooze." He ran his hand along the curve of my spine and let it rest on my bottom. "That's not my scene."

"I know." It really wasn't. He hated social events, but he was going tonight because he loved me and knew how important it was to me. I hadn't been able to hide my excitement when we had received the invitation to the annual fundraising gala hosted every New Year's Eve by Holly's sorority alumnus organization. Although it was shallow as hell, I wanted to be part of the "in" crowd.

Ivan brushed his knuckles along my cheek, and I turned my head to kiss his scarred, tattooed fingers. His expression darkened, and he asked, "Do you want me to cover these?"

Hating that he was so self-conscious about the way people judged me for being married to him, I kissed each gnarled finger. "No."

"Are you sure?" He stared at the bluish-green and black markings. "I don't mind."

"I mind." I lifted up on tiptoes and sought his mouth. "I'm not ashamed of you." He started to protest, and I kissed him again. "I love you. All of you."

He cupped my face and nuzzled his nose against mine before capturing my mouth in a slow and easy kiss. "You're too good for me."

"No, we're just right for each other." Determined to someday convince him that he was absolutely good enough and worthy of love and a family, I slid my arms around his waist and pressed my cheek to his chest. He hugged me tightly, and I wondered, not for the first time, if we should look into some kind of counseling for his deep-seated feelings of unworthiness. Being abandoned as a baby and left to fend for himself in an orphanage that was poorly run, negligent and abusive had left him broken inside. I wished my love was enough to glue together those pieces of him that his childhood had fractured, but I was realizing that it wasn't.

"I have something for you."

Glancing up at him, I studied his face for a moment, trying to decide if he was about to make a sex joke. Narrowing my eyes with suspicion, I asked, "Do I have to put my hand in your pocket to find it?"

He laughed. "You're welcome to put your hand in my pocket anytime, but no." He gestured to the spacious closet we shared. "The top drawer where I keep my watches."

Loving his little surprises, I hurried back to the closet and opened the drawer. The distinctive box from Zoya's shop greeted me, and I glanced back at him with a grin on my face. He had followed me into the closet and leaned against the door frame, smiling indulgently as I giddily opened the box and gasped at the sight of the glittering diamonds bezel-set in rose gold. "Ivan!"

"You were so excited when that invitation came," he explained, closing the distance between us. "I wanted you to have something pretty and new for tonight." He grazed his fingertips over my bare shoulder, and I leaned into his touch. "When you showed me the dress you picked, I went straight to Zoya."

"That little sneak didn't say a word!" I was only a tiny bit annoyed she had kept this a secret. I enjoyed surprises so much I couldn't hold it against her.

"You can take it up with her when you see her later," he suggested, taking the necklace from the box. He swept aside the silky hair of my newly installed extensions and draped the necklace around my neck. "Hopefully, her father won't throw a drink in my face."

I looked up at him and frowned. "I hope you're joking."

His focus remained on the clasp of the necklace as he admitted, "Kazimir was still angry when I picked these up this morning."

"Angry? At you? Why? What happened outside the barre studio wasn't your fault!"

"Zoya's father knows what I am and what I did. He'll never believe that what happened to you and Zoya wasn't my fault."

I huffed. "That's not fair. Maybe I should talk to him."

"No." He managed to get the clasp hooked finally and bent down to kiss the side of my neck. "Let him be angry at me."

"That's not right, Ivan. You didn't do anything."

"Not this time," he replied and took the earrings from the box. When he placed them in my hand, I caught his gaze. I started to say that he didn't have to endure Kazimir's ire as penance for something he had done years ago but decided to let it go—for now.

When I finished putting on the earrings, I moved to the full-length mirror in the corner of my dressing area. Ivan stood behind me, his big, strong hands on my waist. Our reflection made my heart flutter wildly. His crisp, tailored tuxedo fit him to perfection, highlighting his broad shoulders, and the glimmering rose gold and diamonds popped against the simplicity of my black off-the-shoulder gown. My gaze settled on the gleaming black alligator boots I had picked out for him. He had been wearing them around the house for the last few weeks to break them in, and even though he swore up and down he hated them, I could tell he secretly enjoyed them.

He tugged me back against his hard body and noisily kissed my cheek. "Ready for the ball, Cinderella?"

"Yep."

He grabbed the custom black cowboy hat I had insisted he have made and settled it into place. I couldn't help the grin that tugged at the corners of my mouth. He narrowed his eyes. "What?"

"You are going to wear that hat again in March," I decided, stepping closer and sliding my arms around his waist. "You're going to wear those boots and some jeans and a starched shirt and take me out for steak and whiskey before we head over to the rodeo to watch the bull riding."

"And then?" he asked, leaning down to sneak a kiss.

"And then you're going to bring me home, bend me over the couch and—"

He chuckled darkly against my neck and nipped at a sensitive spot that made me shiver. "I think I know what comes next."

"Hopefully me," I said with a giggle at the ticklish kisses he placed along my neck and shoulder. When his hands started to ruck up the sides of my dress, I covered them with my own. "No."

"Yes," he grumbled.

"Later," I insisted and caressed his jaw. "When we get home, you can do whatever you want with me."

His gaze darkened with lust, but his wolfish smile seemed to be hinting at a secret. "We aren't coming home tonight."

A ripple of surprised excitement coursed through me. "No?"

"No." His grin made it clear that he wasn't going to tell me what his plans were for after the gala. Deciding to revel in the anticipation of what he had arranged, I held tight to his hand as he led us out of the house and out to his SUV. My gaze lingered on the empty spot where my car normally sat. The memory of the fire and the attack in the barre studio parking lot flashed before me, and I batted it away, irritated that those ugly thoughts were trying to ruin my night.

"I spoke to Alexei this morning," Ivan said as he helped me into the front seat, holding my skirt to make sure it wasn't caught in the door. "He invited us to come over to one of his lots whenever you're ready."

I made a face. "His cars are so expensive."

"And?"

Recognizing that tone I knew it was pointless to argue with him. Instead, I buckled my seat belt. "We can figure it out later."

He huffed, fully aware I would push back against the idea of dropping an obscene and unnecessary amount of money on a luxury brand, but the gleam in his eyes warned that he had methods—very delicious and naughty methods—of persuading me to see things his way. As he backed out of our garage, I allowed myself to imagine what it might be like to drive an Audi or Jaguar or Mercedes. It would be a huge step up from my base model but very reliable car. Maybe something with more space in the second row to accommodate a car seat and some extra room in the cargo area for a stroller…

Ivan's big, warm hand reached for mine as we idled at a red light. I enjoyed the feel of his fingers and let my thoughts drift to the wonderful and exciting future I hoped the next year held for us. I wanted that for my sister, too. I wanted Ruby to leave jail and thrive, to move on from the bad decisions she had made and start a new and better chapter in her life. I wanted to build a family with Ivan that included Ruby as a doting, present aunt.

But, first, I had to get her out of whatever trouble she had stumbled into this time.

CHAPTER SIX

A FTER LEAVING THE SUV with the valet, Ivan took my arm and escorted me into the Post Oak Hotel. I grinned at Ivan as we stepped into reception area outside the grand ballroom and joined the line for our seating assignments. When we entered the ballroom, it was everything I had imagined it would be and giddily grabbed Ivan's hand, practically dragging him into the party.

Lena and Yuri found us almost as soon as we entered the room. Vivian and Nikolai wandered over a short time later with Alexei and his new wife, Shay. We had been at their elopement in Vegas a few months earlier and had been at their home for Thanksgiving. Shay was quickly becoming one of my favorite new friends. As we drank champagne and enjoyed the hors d'oeuvres offered by the passing waitstaff, we looked over the tables of silent auction items.

"No surprise here," Vivian remarked, tapping the list of bids for one of Zoya's necklaces.

"No," I agreed and sipped my champagne.

Next to us, Lena slipped her arm under Shay's and asked, "See anything you want your man to buy you?"

Shay shyly shook her head. "I've got everything I need."

"Yes, but what do you *want*?" Lena insisted as she led Shay to the next table laden with outrageously expensive vacations.

"Should we intervene or let her corrupt Shay?" Vivian asked with a smile as we remained behind.

"Let her corrupt," I laughed softly. "Alexei is like Yuri. He shows his love with gifts. He'll be over the moon if she asks him for something expensive." I moved toward a different table where a piece of sports memorabilia had caught my eye. Knowing how much Ivan loved the Rockets, I couldn't pass up the chance to bid on a few items from players he watched almost religiously. Vivian touched my arm, letting me know she was leaving to rejoin her husband, and I smiled at her before turning my attention back to the items I wanted.

After jotting down my bids and noting the closing time for each piece, I wandered around the remaining tables looking for anything else interesting. I slowed down and stopped to read the description for a Napa Valley vacation package that included a hot air balloon ride. My thoughts turned away from the ritzy glamour of the gala to my sister sitting in her cold jail cell, counting down the days and hours until her release. Ruby had always wanted to go for a ride in a hot air balloon. She used to ask for a ride in one every year on her birthday, but our parents had never arranged it.

But I can.

It would have to wait until after she completed her probation and was allowed to travel outside of the county. We could make it a girls-only trip and reconnect away from our everyday lives. Maybe not Napa Valley. She used to talk about Sedona so maybe Arizona…

"Erin?"

The familiar voice of my ex-boyfriend Teague cut through

my thoughts. We had ended things on good terms almost a year before I met Ivan and I still enjoyed his company the few times we had crossed paths. Turning toward him, I smiled up at him. "Hello, Teague."

When he moved in for a hug, I allowed it because he had never been anything but respectful of the boundaries of our friendship since the breakdown of our relationship. I was taken aback by the scent of bourbon and cigarettes clinging to him as we hugged. He had never smoked and only rarely had a beer when we dated. As we pulled apart, I noticed the stress lines around his eyes and mouth. Considering the long hours his job required, I wasn't too surprised. Gently, I asked, "Rough time at work?"

He looked chagrined and rubbed at his jaw. "The cigarettes, huh?"

I nodded. "And the bourbon."

He made a face. "Sorry. I, uh, got started a little early this year." He rubbed the back of his neck. "The cigarettes are a bad habit I picked up from some of the guys on my floor at the firm."

"Well, I'm not going to nag you about them," I promised. "Tonight, at least."

He laughed. "Thank goodness you're in a festive mood tonight."

"There are other firms you could work at," I suggested.

"Not for the kind of money I'm making now." His answer didn't surprise me. If anything, it was a clear reminder of why we hadn't worked. "I like where I'm at, and there are some clear paths to the C-suite at my firm. The bonuses can't be beat."

"As long as you're happy there," I replied, choosing not to say what I was really thinking. His issues with his work-life balance weren't my problem anymore.

"And you? Are you happy working for your husband?" His tone was yet another reminder of why we hadn't worked out together. "Seems like a waste of your degree and all those certifications to work as his secretary."

"First of all," I stepped toward him, "I worked *with* my husband. Secondly, I am using my degree."

"And third?" He arched his blond brows.

"I don't have to justify my career choices to anyone." Handing him my empty champagne flute, I turned on my heel and walked away from him. Irritated that I let him get under my skin, I breathed out my frustration. Before I even cast a glance around the room to find Ivan, I felt his comforting hand settle against the small of my back. His familiar warmth radiated through my dress and into my skin. My eyes closed for a brief and perfect moment as he tenderly kissed my cheek and then my neck.

"Do you want me to kick his ass?" His deep, rumbling voice was barely loud enough for me to hear. He slid his arm around my waist and tugged me in tight to his side. "I know that look on your face. What did he say?"

"Nothing important," I assured him. "He just wanted to remind me why I dumped him."

He grumbled something under his breath and then clasped my hand. "Let's go find our seats. The dinner is about to start."

We found our table in the middle section of the ballroom. There was already a couple sitting there I didn't recognize, but the sudden tightening of Ivan's hand around mine told me that he did. There wasn't enough time for him to tell me what was wrong because the couple stood and introduced themselves.

"James," Ivan said, reaching out to shake the man's hand. "This is my wife, Erin."

"Pleasure to meet you, Erin." His grip was stiff around mine, and I had the immediate sensation that he was hiding something. He let go of my hand and gestured to the gorgeous blonde next to him. "This is my wife, Missy."

"Nice to meet you, Missy." I clasped her hand and noticed the swell of her midsection under her glitzy red dress, but I didn't congratulate her for fear of making a terrible faux pas.

"Oh, you can say it," Missy said, clearly noticing my gaze. "Five months," she clarified. "Our sixth."

"Another boy," James said proudly and kissed his wife's temple.

"Congratulations," I said with a genuine smile. "That's an incredible blessing."

"Do you two have children?" Missy asked, and Ivan's hand moved to my hip, giving me a reassuring squeeze.

"Not yet." I smiled up at Ivan. "But we're working on it."

"Practice makes perfect," James said as he held out his wife's chair.

Ivan mirrored his movements and held out mine, his fingertips grazing my bare shoulders as he took his seat next to me. Other couples started to make their way to the empty seats at our table and the ones surrounding us. I noticed Lena and Yuri walking toward the front where they sat near Vivian and Nikolai. Alexei and Shay were right beside us at a table filled with couples that he clearly knew very well judging by all the smiles and laughs.

Ivan straightened with obvious interest when the last couple joined our table and sat in the last two seats by him. I recognized the basketball player, Amos, and Karima, his hotshot attorney wife, from TV and social media. James and his wife had a strange reaction to the couple joining our eight-top. Their smiles seemed strained and obviously forced, and their handshakes were quick. Ivan, on the other hand, didn't even hide his enthusiasm as he greeted them, and I wasn't at all surprised that Amos immediately started asking him about open training slots at the warehouse.

"So, you work with your husband?" James asked as he shifted to the side to allow a waiter to pour wine in his glass.

"Yes." I covered my glass with my hand, indicating I wanted water with my meal. My head already felt a little light after the champagne. "I handle the business side of the gym."

"Do you also train with him?" Missy asked. "It's just that I noticed you have some stitches," she said and gestured toward her hairline. "I thought it might have been a gym accident."

"Oh. No." I self-consciously adjusted my bangs to cover them again. "Actually, I was mugged outside a barre studio. A random robbery. I fell and hit my head," I explained, keeping the details to myself and waving off their concern. "I'm totally fine, though."

"What is happening to this city?" Missy asked with a huff. "I swear every time I turn on the news it's a story about a robbery or a murder or some kind of assault." She shook her head. "We need more police on the streets to handle these gangs and lowlife thugs."

Not wanting to debate her on the topics of policing or gang violence or the cycle of poverty, I was relieved when her husband redirected the conversation after a stern look her way. "So, you don't train at the gym?" he asked, his expression softening when he looked back at me.

"Not in BJJ," I clarified. "I use the gym for cardio and some light lifting, but that's it. There aren't any fighters at the gym close enough to my weight or size to make it safe to wrestle on the mats."

"No women at the gym?" Missy frowned.

"Just me." It was one of the issues we argued about on a regular basis. I wanted to open up the gym to women, but Ivan refused because he wasn't comfortable training them.

"Seems like you're losing out on a big chunk of business," James remarked. "Lots of women are into MMA these days."

"They sure are," I agreed. "The Connolly brothers have lots of classes for women and kids. There are a few other gyms in the area that offer them, too. We're just not one of them."

"I heard there was some interest about the Warehouse hosting a camp for that fighter show on TV," James said, clearly aware that it was more than simple interest.

"We've had some discussions." Not wanting to get into the nitty gritty details of a deal that hadn't been ironed out yet, I changed the subject. "So, what do you two do?"

"I'm a stay at home mom. I also homeschool the boys and run a blog and YouTube channel."

"Oh wow! You must be exhausted when bedtime rolls around," I said, unable to imagine wrangling five rambunctious boys while pregnant and working.

"I am, but it's all worth it. My boys deserve the best." She smiled warmly and rubbed her husband's arm. "We want them to be raised in a good Christian home with traditional family values. We don't want them exposed to the wrong ideas."

I suspected the wrong ideas might be things like evolution but didn't want to get into that deep of a discussion at a charity dinner. Instead, I said, "I had friends at college who were homeschooled. They all did extremely well."

"Did you go to the public schools here?" she asked.

I shook my head. "I went to St. John's. My sister and I both went there," I clarified. "Our mother was the CFO at the school."

"And your father?" James asked.

"He was a partner at Ernst & Young," I explained, hoping they would let the issue drop soon. I wasn't in the mood to bring up my dead parents tonight. "And what do you do, James?"

"I'm in real estate. I own a commercial development company headquartered in Dallas, but I've opened a new branch here."

"Are you working on the I-45 widening project?"

"We are," he confirmed. Then, with a knowing smile, he asked, "Why? Do you have some property you want to develop?"

"Maybe," I answered coyly. "I know tonight isn't the time to talk business, though."

"No," he agreed, "but it's a good time to make connections. We could schedule a meeting later this week? You can find my details online at our business site."

"Sure." I turned away from James for a brief moment as Ivan squeezed my thigh under the table to get my attention.

We shared a look that easily communicated what he wanted me to know. *That man is dangerous. Don't promise him anything.* I found his hand under the tablecloth and squeezed it to let him know I understood.

As the appetizer courses arrived, the hostesses of the night took the stage. I glanced around the room, expecting to see Holly somewhere but the table where her mother sat had two empty seats. Maybe she wasn't in the mood to celebrate after her ordeal in Mexico…

When the dancing started after dinner, Ivan wasted no time tugging me out to the center of the room. We had been working on his two-step since the invitation arrived, and he proved how quickly he mastered new skills as he shuffled us around the room to a George Strait cover band. We hadn't danced this much since Bianca and Sergei's wedding, and it felt so good to let loose and have fun.

Just after eleven, I stopped by the auction tables to see if my bids had won. I managed to contain my squeal of excitement when I saw that I had won two of the items I wanted for Ivan. Now I just had to figure out how to surprise him with them.

"I think we're going to head on home," Vivian said as she joined me near the sports memorabilia table. She rested her hands on her very pregnant belly and sighed. "I am beat."

"Go home. Make Nikolai massage your feet." I glanced at her heels and shook my head. "I don't know how you're walking in those things."

"Very carefully," she said with a laugh. She hugged me good night and turned to leave. "I'll see you tomorrow at brunch."

"Yep." Scanning the room for Ivan, I found him talking to some similarly tall, burly types. Athletes. Probably interested in joining the gym and rolling around on the mats with Ivan and his team. As if he could feel my gaze, he glanced my way, and I touched my earlobe, our secret signal that I was running off to the ladies room. He nodded, and I blew him a dramatic kiss. He grinned, and I pivoted on my heel, walking away with a little extra swing to my hips. The night was winding down, and I knew my husband well enough to expect a wild romp once he had me alone again.

The line for the bathroom was longer than I had expected, and I had a few moments to open my clutch and check my phone. There were the usual social media notifications and texts wishing me a happy new year. A missed phone call caught my eye. I didn't recognize the number. There was a voicemail, too.

Certain it was someone who had drunk dialed the wrong number, I left it unopened and tucked my phone back into my clutch. The line moved more quickly, and in no time at all, I was standing at the sink washing my hands. I kept hold of my paper towel as I reached the door, using it to grab the handle and catching the door with the toe of my shoe before tossing the paper towel in the nearby trash.

Out in the dim but warmly lit hallway, I sidestepped a trio of women consoling a crying fourth and averted my gaze when I passed an older couple making out like teenagers in a dark corner. Alcohol had been free flowing all night, and people were starting to get loose with their behavior. It was amusing to say the least.

"Erin."

I cringed inwardly at the sound of Teague's voice. With an aggrieved sigh, I turned toward him. "Teague."

He swayed on his feet, and I worried he was about to topple over onto his face. He had lost his bowtie and vest sometime during the night, and his cowboy hat was crumpled in his left hand. His cheeks were ruddy and his eyes were glassy as he stepped toward me with an accusatory finger. "I know your secret."

Taken aback, I asked, "What secret?"

"About your sister," he slurred.

I rolled my eyes. "You're drunk. Call for a ride. Go home. Sleep it off."

"You better do what they told you, sweetheart. Tell your sister to keep her mouth shut—or else."

A cold chill coursed through my body, freezing me right to the very spot I stood. "What did you say?"

"You heard me." He poked my shoulder hard enough that I winced, and I stepped back to get away from him. He stepped forward, boxing me in against the wall. His sour breath assaulted my nose as he leaned down and stage whispered, "You can lie all you want to the cops, but I know the truth. I know what your sister did, and I know what they're going to do to you if she talks." His expression slackened as he grew suddenly sad. "The same thing they're going to do to me."

Ignoring the warning bells inside my head that urged me to flee, I asked, "Who is they?"

He shook his head and wagged his finger right in my face. "No, ma'am. I'm not saying a word." He mimicked zipping his lips. "Then they'll really fuck me up."

"I'm two seconds away from fucking you up," Ivan

snarled, seeming to appear from thin air. He gripped Teague's shoulder and spun him around, pushing him up against the wall. Looking down at Teague, he growled, "If you ever touch my wife again, I'll cut off both your fucking hands. Understand?"

Teague shoved at Ivan, but it was useless against a man so much stronger and taller. "Fuck off, you big Russian asshole." He shoved Ivan with both hands this time, but Ivan didn't move. "I had my hands all over your wife before you ever did." He leered at me. "Not just my hands. My dick was—"

He didn't get a chance to finish his filthy statement. In a flash, Ivan spun him around and yanked his arm behind his back. He used his greater height and strength to push Teague flat against the wall, smashing the side of his face against the glimmering gold wallpaper. He moved his mouth close to Teague's ear and said something I couldn't hear. Whatever it was, Teague paled and nodded rapidly.

A second later, Ivan whirled him away from the wall and shoved him down the hallway. He clenched his fists at his side, and I placed a hand on his chest, feeling his heart pounding against his sternum and his lungs expanding with amped up breaths. I rubbed his chest and drew his attention away from a scurrying Teague to me. He covered my hand with his, and I smiled gently. "Let's go."

He didn't have to be asked twice. Leaving behind his hat somewhere in the main ballroom, he led me not to the valet stand outside as I expected but to the elevator bank. I shot him a questioning look, and he shrugged as if to say, "Trust me." So I did.

We stepped into the next elevator, and he reached into his

tuxedo jacket to retrieve his wallet. He pulled a hotel card key from it and scanned it. The elevator doors closed, and we started moving up toward the exclusive floors of the hotel. When the elevator stopped, he gave my hand a playful tug and led me to one of two doors on the entire floor. He unlocked our room and gestured for me to walk inside first.

Giddy with anticipation, I entered the opulent foyer and spun around to face my grinning husband. "Ivan!"

"So you like it?"

"Yes!"

"Good." He shut the door and locked it behind him before closing the distance between us with long, determined strides. The soles of his boots tapped against the marble tile, and my heart raced as his heated gaze promised a night of wild bliss. His hands settled on my hips, and he bent down to nuzzle my cheek and then my neck.

"Why?"

"Because you deserve it," he answered matter-of-factly. His big hands moved to the side of my dress where he had helped me zip up earlier. He lowered it slowly while dotting ticklish kisses along my bare shoulder. "I know it's been hard for you. The robbery. Your sister." He hesitated. "Our baby project."

My eyes closed as he pushed my gown down my arms. Even though I wanted to get lost in the romantic moment, I realized we had to talk about what had happened downstairs. "About Teague—"

"No," he interrupted gruffly. "I don't want to hear his name again."

"But he said—"

Ivan pulled back enough to gaze down into my eyes. "Is it something we can fix tonight?"

I shook my head. "No."

"Then let's leave it until tomorrow," he urged and then kissed the protest right out of me. He pushed the dress down my body, skimming his hands over the swaths of naked skin he uncovered. He let loose an appreciative growl when I stood in only my thong, bra, jewelry and heels. "Don't move."

I didn't dare. Standing there in the entryway, I watched him undress, peeling off layer after layer until he was barefoot in his boxer briefs. He reminded me of a lion as he stalked toward me. I trembled inside, trying to decide if I should run and make him chase me or stay right there and let him devour me.

I chose the latter.

He pushed me back against the closest wall and dragged my tiny thong down my thighs and legs until I could step out of it. He wasted no time getting what he wanted after that. He lifted my left leg and draped it over his shoulder, giving him the access he needed. He attacked my pussy like a starving man, shocking me with the insistent swipe of his tongue.

I started to sway, and he grabbed my other leg, lifting it up over his shoulder. He gripped my ass with one hand while the other stroked between my cheeks and then dipped into my wet heat. His tongue did incredible things to me, licking and flicking at my clit with just the right speed and pressure. He had learned and mastered my body and used that knowledge to drive me wild.

"No!" I cried out in protest when he pulled his mouth away from me. I was so close my legs were shaking. He smiled up at me and wiped his wet mouth on my belly. He lowered my legs and rose to his full height, towering over me and reminding me how big and strong he was. As if he wanted to drive that point home, he swept me up into his arms and carried me bridal style to the incredible bedroom of the suite.

Champagne. Roses. Pastries. Fruit. He had arranged for a romantic setup, and my heart almost burst with my love for him. "Ivan!"

"I planned to drink champagne first, but I can't wait," he admitted.

"It will keep," I assured him.

He grinned at my enthusiasm and lowered me carefully to the bed. He covered my body with his, sharing his heat and warming me right up. His hands roamed my body, stroking and squeezing until I was panting with need. His thick fingers traced my labia, dipping between and swirling around my clit. He slid one finger and then two more deep inside me, stretching me and stroking inside for that spot that made me gasp. When he found it, I arched off the bed. "Ivan!"

"I want you to come for me," he ordered before capturing my mouth. "I want you to soak my hand with your cum. Get so wet my dick slides right in, so you can take all of it, balls deep."

"Ivan!" I gripped his wrist as he fingered me faster and faster. He moved his thumb over my clit, letting it rub against my swollen pearl with every thrust of his wrist. I was obscenely wet now, my body dripping for him and the promise of that huge cock. My thighs tensed, and I dug my toes into the soft bedding. He kissed me roughly, forcing his tongue between my lips, and I lost it. With a guttural groan, I did exactly as he asked. I came hard and soaked his hand.

I was still shaking and trembling with the aftershocks of my orgasm when he flipped me over, tossing me around on the bed and shoving my knees forward to cant my ass higher. The bed moved as he jerked down his boxer briefs and threw them. I screamed in shock when I felt his tongue, not his cock, on my pussy. "Ivan!"

He gripped the backs of my thighs and buried his face in me. My embarrassment at being licked like this faded quickly when his tongue settled over my clit. At that point, I lost all inhibition. He could do whatever he wanted as long as he kept fluttering his tongue right there.

When I started to pant and shake, he pulled his face away from me, drawing a moan of protest from my throat. He grabbed my hips and rubbed his shaft against my slick heat. With a forceful thrust, he buried his entire length inside me. I cried out at the shock and relief of being filled by him. "Ivan! Please!"

"Please what?" He gripped my hair in one big hand and tugged my head back. "Please what?"

"Fuck me," I begged. "Fuck me hard." I reached back and scratched at his thigh, desperate to get him deeper. "Wreck me."

He growled like a bear and gave me exactly what I wanted. He took complete control, unleashing that beast within him that I craved more than any other. I would be sore in the morning, and I would probably have bruises on my hips and shoulders from his tight grasp. I wanted them. I wanted to see my reflection in the mirror and know that Ivan enjoyed my body so much he left his mark on me.

His thumb suddenly breached my bottom, and I gasped at the wild sensation of being penetrated in both places. I couldn't help myself. I reached down between my legs and ran my hand along my vulva and then over his shaft to his testicles. He swore in Russian, filthy words falling off his tongue as I made him crazy by touching him in such an unexpected way.

Ready to come and hoping he was ready to go with me, I moved my fingers to my clit and touched myself. It didn't take much to get me close and even less to push me over the edge. I screamed my husband's name, begging him not to stop, begging him to keep going, and he obliged. He gripped my shoulders in both hands and drove into me, pushing me down against the mattress as he chased his own release.

"Erin," he growled. "*Solnyshka. Angel.*" He thrust deep and held still, his shaft throbbing inside me as he pumped me full of his seed. I panted beneath him, completely limp and satisfied. Unable to move, I let him turn me over and drag me onto his chest. I trembled with aftershocks, and he stroked my back and hair. "Happy New Year, baby."

Sleepy and content, I murmured, "Happy New Year, Ivan."

CHAPTER SEVEN

EVEN ON A day when he was supposed to be enjoying some well-earned relaxation, Ivan couldn't sleep longer than seven. His internal clock wouldn't allow it. Not ready to get out of bed just yet, he turned onto his side and faced Erin. She was a deep sleeper. He swore a train could barrel through their bedroom and she wouldn't even twitch.

The early morning fog in his mind cleared away as he remembered the run-in with Teague. His jaw clenched at the memory of that asshole forcing Erin against a wall and taunting her made his gut burn with anger. It had taken every ounce of restraint not to hit him last night. Had he been younger and wilder, less afraid of consequence, he would have unleashed hell on Teague's face, but he was older now, married and understood that he had so much to lose.

Whatever Teague had said to Erin had rattled her. He felt some guilt at not letting her tell him last night, but he had planned everything for a romantic escape to make her feel special. He hadn't wanted Teague to ruin the rest of their night.

Now, though, he wanted to know what Teague had said. He also wanted to know if Teague had treated her like that when they were together. Neither of them talked about their past lovers much. None of his relationships before Erin had ever lasted more than a few weeks, and she had confessed to never loving anyone until him. She had cared for the men in her past, but she swore that he was the only one who ever awakened feelings of actual love. He believed her. Losing her parents and having an older sister who struggled with addiction had left her aloof and afraid to be vulnerable. Maybe she had sensed the same thing in him. Maybe that was what had drawn them together that fateful day she had walked into his gym and asked for his help.

Not wanting to wake her, he rested his head on his palm and simply enjoyed the view. In quiet moments like these, he couldn't quite believe that she belonged to him. He couldn't fathom how a woman like this could ever love him. She deserved so much more than he was able to give her, but she seemed to be entirely content with the life they were building together.

He tried not to doubt her love for him. He tried not to let the wounds of his childhood ruin the wonderful gift that he had been given. He had spent so much of his life being unworthy, unwanted and unloved that it was still difficult to adjust to Erin telling him every single day how much she loved and cared for him. That someone so sweet and kind and generous and unmarred by the darkness of life could want him—could cherish and love him—was jarring.

But she did.

The little things he did to make her smile and feel special, the unexpected gifts or surprise getaways like this one, were like an insurance policy. The scared little boy inside him who feared being abandoned believed that giving her gifts and making her life comfortable would balance out any of the stupid things he might say or do to lessen her love for him. He hated that he felt that way. He believed her when she said she didn't need or want expensive things, but it didn't stop him from enjoying her excited smile at receiving something pretty. Her joy in receiving his gifts was matched in his joy in giving them.

Overcome with need, he leaned down and gently kissed her lips. He brushed his fingers along her cheek and jaw and pressed another kiss at the side of her mouth. She inhaled deeply and snuggled into him, her elegant hands reaching for his waist and shoulder. He combed his fingers through her hair and captured her mouth in a more determined kiss. She whimpered against his tongue, and his cock pulsed to life.

She sighed happily as he rolled her onto her back, covering her petite body and pushing her legs apart with his knees. He ran his hand down her side to her hip and then swept along her inner thigh until he reached her pussy. She arched into his touch, and he smiled against her mouth. With the practiced ease of a man who knew his wife's body, he stroked between her thighs until his fingers were slick with her wet heat.

She grew impatient and hooked her heels against the backs of his thighs, tugging him toward her. He didn't need to be asked twice. He reached down and guided himself into her, and she moaned needily. Her short nails scratched his shoulders as she clung to him, taking his slow and steady strokes. It was the sort of unhurried lovemaking that he had never imagined he would enjoy until her. He liked to take his time and draw out both their pleasures.

She brought her own hand between their bodies. The sight

of her slim fingers rubbing fast circles around her clit made his breath hitch. Usually she liked it when he touched her, but this morning she was so excited she couldn't wait. He moved his hand from her breast to her neck, running his thumb along the front of her throat in a way that made her pupils dilate. He would never take it beyond a gentle caress of her neck—*never*—but she enjoyed the slight reminder of the command and power he had over her.

He let his hand drift higher until his thumb was between her lips, and the rest of his fingers curled around her jaw and cheek. Her thighs tightened around his waist, and she stroked herself faster. A flush spread across her chest and crept into her neck and her face as she panted. Her eyes shut briefly and then she gasped. "Ivan!"

Feeling her come undone under him killed his control. He fell forward, planting his arm next to her head and using his other hand to grab her ass and shift the angle. She cried out pleasure, and he snapped his hips, fucking into her while she clutched at his hips and waist and shoulders.

"I love you," she whispered against his cheek. Her lips touched his skin, and he shuddered at the wild feelings she evoked. "I love you so much."

That was all it took to push him over the edge. He gripped the back of her neck, tangling his fingers in her hair, and captured her mouth in a punishing kiss as he came. She moaned and stroked his back, easing him down from the high of his climax.

Reluctant to move away from her, he stayed buried inside her until he slipped out, taking advantage of their closeness to kiss her until her lips were swollen. He dropped onto his side and slipped an arm under her waist, dragging her across the bed until she was trapped in his embrace. She giggled at the caveman move and kissed his jaw. "That was the perfect way to start this new year."

He smiled as he combed his fingers through her hair. "I feel guilty about waking you up early."

"It's okay. I can nap later."

"We have the room until tomorrow. You should visit the spa."

"I might see if they have any openings after our brunch date."

He groaned at the reminder. "Is it at Samovar?"

She snorted and patted his chest. "No. Lena refused, and Vivian finally agreed to let Benny choose the spot."

"Finally," he grumbled.

She laughed and lightly scratched her nails down his chest to just under his navel and then back up again. After a few moments of idle stroking, she gently asked, "Can we talk about Teague?"

"Yes." He covered her hand with his and turned to look at her. "What did he say that upset you?"

"He knew."

"About?"

"About the parking lot."

"I don't understand."

"He knew what they said to me." His heart skipped a beat, and he studied her face. Fear and confusion were reflected in her eyes. "How could he know that if he wasn't there or involved in some way?"

"He wouldn't," Ivan agreed, his mind racing with possibilities. "I don't want you to see him again. He's dangerous."

"I don't want to see him again," she assured him. "There was something…off about him last night."

"Off? How?"

"He was drunk. He smelled like cigarettes. He looked stressed."

"What does he do? Something with money?"

"Investment banking," she clarified. "He's a killer," she emphasized. "He has an affinity for it. For the risk," she explained.

"Maybe he took too much risk with someone else's money," he suggested.

"Probably," she agreed, "but how in the world is his job connected to Ruby in jail?"

"I don't know." He didn't like not knowing. It made him uneasy and tense. "But I'll find out."

"I can do a little digging," she offered. "One of my friends from college works at the firm."

He wanted to forbid it, but she would only go behind his back and that would put her in even more danger. "Carefully," he said finally. "Very, very carefully."

"I promise." She shifted in closer until her cheek was against his chest. After a moment, she asked, "What's the deal with the Muellers?"

"He's the head of a white supremacist group."

"What?" Aghast, she lifted her head and frowned. "Seriously?"

He nodded. "He's the respectable side of those crazy, hateful fucks. The side with the money and the connections that makes them all dangerous."

She cringed and groaned. "Oh my God! No wonder they made that face when Amos and Karima sat down!" She looked at her hand and made a face. "Ew! I touched them both!"

"I don't think you can catch hatred like a germ, *angel moy*."

She rolled her pretty eyes. "Obviously! I just mean that I sort of enjoyed their company. Not like I want to be friends or anything, but I thought they were okay. Now, I find out they're tiki-torch-wielding white power weirdos!"

"Well, we don't ever have to see them again."

"We might," she countered. "If you want to develop some of your property—"

"Our property," he corrected.

"Our property," she amened. "We may have to deal with him. I already said I would make a meeting with him."

"Go to the meeting. See what he has to say. When it's over, pretend you're thinking about it. Give it a day or two to think it over and tell him no. Diplomatically," he added. "The last thing we need is problems with someone like that."

"What about Ruby? I'm worried. I still haven't heard from her."

"She's probably being shuffled between parts of the jail." He wanted to ease her fears, but secretly, he worried something bad had happened to her sister. "A lot of prisoners reaching the end of their stretch get moved from one cell block to another or to ad seg."

"I'm sure that's it," Erin said softly. "I'll be glad when we get her home."

He didn't share those feelings. "I know you will."

She pressed a kiss to his jaw and slowly untangled herself

from his arms and the sheet. "Want to take a shower with me?"

"Like you have to ask?" He swung his legs over the side of the bed and stood. He stretched, and his stomach growled loudly. Rubbing his hand over his abs, he admitted, "I'm starving."

"Of course, you are! You didn't have your giant tumbler of protein sludge, your gallon of water and twenty eggs."

"It's not sludge," he grumbled. "And I've never eaten twenty eggs in one sitting."

She patted his empty stomach and then gave his backside a swat. "I'll order some room service before I hop in with you. We'll be dressed when it gets here."

He stole a quick kiss and pinched her bottom in retribution for the swat. She squealed and playfully smacked his hand. Laughing, he strode to the bathroom and turned on the shower, adjusting the heat of the various heads until they felt right. He took advantage of the privacy to relieve himself and then stepped into the shower. He had barely gotten his head and shoulders wet when Erin barged into the bathroom. "Ivan!"

"What's wrong?" He shoved aside the sliding glass door and stepped onto the bath mat where she stood with her phone in her hand.

"Last night, I had a call from a number I didn't recognize. I assumed it was a misdial or a spam call, but listen." She held out the phone and tapped the speaker icon on the screen.

He recoiled at the sound of a woman screaming. His initial assumption that it was Ruby screaming was quickly dashed when the woman started begging for help in Spanish. Her pained cries and the slap of something—a belt, he thought—against her body echoed in the bathroom. There was no mistaking the grunting in the background. His stomach turned at the realization they were listening to a rape.

The voicemail ended mid-scream. Erin's hand shook as she lowered her phone. She looked ready to crumble, and he quickly grabbed her around the waist, hauling her against his soaking wet body to keep her upright. He pressed his face to hers and hurriedly assured her, "It's not Ruby. You know that, right?"

"I know," she said, starting to cry.

"It's just some asshole trying to scare you."

"It's working."

He clenched his jaw, hating that his wife was being tormented like this.

"What if that's been happening to Ruby?"

Hearing her voice his concern didn't make it any easier for him to say, "It's possible."

"Do you think that's what she saw? What they want her to be quiet about?"

"It could be," he confirmed reluctantly. "Or, it might be some sick bastard who is taunting you."

"I need to call her lawyer."

He started to tell her that there was nothing Ruby's lawyer could do. There was no way to prove the call had any link to her sister. Ruby was getting out in just under forty-eight hours. Her lawyer wouldn't be able to bust her out any earlier, no matter how much of a fit Erin threw. Instead of telling her that, he said, "If it will make you feel better, call him. See what he says."

She started to tug away, but he held fast. "After our shower. It's not even eight yet. He's probably asleep, and he may not even answer this early in the morning on a holiday."

She relented and placed her phone on the counter. Holding tight to her hand, he led her into the shower. He wanted to anchor her back to reality, to take her thoughts away from the horrible images that voicemail had ignited. Carefully, tenderly, he washed her hair and her body. There was nothing sexual about the act. It was simply a husband cleaning his wife in the gentlest way possible.

But even as he touched her with compassion and love, his mind was turned to darkness and violence. When he caught up with the monster tormenting Erin, he was going to unleash the hateful, cruel side of him that had been caged so very long.

CHAPTER EIGHT

WITH A KNOT of anxiety wobbling in my stomach, I walked through the guest room one last time. I tugged the ends of the comforter and smoothed away the few creases, and fluffed all the pillows. I karate chopped the throw pillow in the reading chair I had picked out for Ruby and rearranged the plush chenille blanket. I stepped into the closet and did a mental inventory of what I had placed on hangers and in the drawers.

Another quiver of anxiety pierced my belly as I worried Ruby would flip out when she realized I had gone shopping for her. After she had gone to jail, I had gone to the apartment she had shared with her boyfriend. By then, the management company had evicted them, and everything was thrown in garbage bags in storage. Lena and Vivian had helped me sort through the bags, picking through the absolutely filthy contents to find what little could be salvaged. Ivan had taken Andrei's things to his family—a few photos, his wallet, his fighting gear, his guitar—and everything else had gone straight to the trash.

The memory of how my sister had been living hurt to remember. Hopped up on pills and meth and whatever else she could get her hands on, she hadn't been eating or showering.

There had been piles of rotting garbage and towers of empty soda and energy drink cans all over the place. The apartment had been so badly damaged that the management company had been preparing to sue her. I had quietly taken care of the bill with my HEMS payout from the trust our parents left behind. Lena had wanted me to send a bill to the trustee to get the money from Ruby's cut, but I didn't care about the fairness of it all. I just wanted it done and over with so we could move on as a family.

"The room is perfect," Ivan remarked when I emerged from the closet. He leaned against the door frame, his thick arms crossed in front of his chest as he watched me. Instead of his usual shorts and tee, he wore dark jeans and a steel gray t-shirt. Shoving off the door, he said, "If she doesn't like it, she can take a Lyft to the closest Motel 6."

"Ivan!" I thumped his chest. "Be nice."

He grumbled and lowered his mouth to mine. "I'll be nice if she's nice."

I rolled my eyes and ducked away from his kiss. "We aren't little kids, Ivan. We can be nice even if she's being a jerk. And she probably is going to be difficult," I added. "The book I've been reading about reuniting with a loved one after prison says that the initial adjustment period to life outside of confinement can be very stressful. I can show you the section."

"I'm sure you highlighted it," he teased. "It would be easy to find if I wanted to read it."

"But you don't want to read it?"

"I don't need a book to tell me about life after prison," he replied testily.

"I wouldn't either if you would talk to me about your time

inside."

"That's not something you want to hear."

"Yes, it is."

"It's not something I want to share."

I bit back the urge to be rude. Instead, I calmly replied, "The book says that most people who spend time in prison don't want to talk to their loved ones about their experience. They don't want to feel weak or vulnerable. They don't want to be forced to justify their actions inside, especially if they had to make difficult choices to survive long enough to get released."

He frowned. "That's not what—"

"If you ever want to talk about that part of your life," I interrupted, determined to get this out, "I will listen to whatever you have to tell me. Without judgment or expectation," I added as a promise.

He gently covered my hand, trapping it over his heart. His expression softened as his other hand cupped the back of my neck. "Thank you for the offer."

This time, when he leaned down for a kiss, I welcomed his mouth on mine. I understood that he would likely never speak to me about what he had endured. There were probably parts of his incarceration that he had sworn never to reveal as part of his oath to the crime family he had served since his adolescence. I was glad that he understood that I would listen if he ever wanted to unburden himself.

"We should go." He checked his watch. "Her lawyer said to get there early."

"I'm ready." After that horrible voicemail, I had contacted Ruby's lawyer to do a welfare check on her. He had charged an outrageous holiday fee to do it, but he had managed to get in to see her that afternoon. He reported that she looked healthy and safe and was ready to get out of there. I had been reassured by his report, but I wouldn't relax until we had her safely in our SUV.

"Is this the bag?" He gestured toward the tote bag I had packed for Ruby.

"Yep."

He picked it up and glanced inside. With a laugh, he pulled out a box and asked, "Pop Tarts are essential?"

"Yes." I took the box from him and dropped it back inside the bag. "She couldn't get blueberry inside."

"And the Dr. Pepper?"

"It's her favorite."

"Was that one of our hoodies?"

"She might be cold when she gets out," I reasoned. "And, anyway, we have a box of them. It's not like they're collectibles or anything."

"Did you remember to charge her new phone?"

"Yes."

"And the old one?"

"It's up in her room."

"Come here." He held out his scarred, tattooed hand and beckoned me closer. I let him draw me in, still feeling annoyed with his teasing. He embraced me tightly and kissed the top of my head. "You and that big heart of yours." He kissed my cheek. "Ruby is lucky to have you for a sister." He kissed the tip of my nose, making me smile. "I'm lucky to have you for a wife."

"Damn right you are," I grumbled before letting him kiss me senseless. When we finally separated, he slid his hand to the small of my back and walked me toward the mud room and into the garage. He held open the passenger door behind my seat so I could stow the bag there and then helped me into my seat, keeping his hand on my bottom way longer than necessary. "Hands to yourself, mister."

"Not a fucking chance," he said in that gruff way that made my heart race and my belly flip-flop with excitement. He swooped in for one more quick kiss before shutting my door and walking around to the driver's side.

"Do you know where we're going?" I asked after I buckled my seat belt. "I can Waze the directions."

Ivan shot me an amused look. "*Milaya moya*, really?"

"Oh. Right." Abashed, I put my phone away. "Obviously, you know where to go."

"It's on Commerce, over by Buffalo Bayou." He backed out of the garage and waited for the door to close before pulling away from the house. "It's an ugly red brick building. There's a sally port where she'll walk out when they release her."

"What is a sally port?"

"It's like a loading dock or a garage entrance to a jail or some other heavily defended place," he explained. "I think it started way back with forts and castles. It was a way to control who got in and out of your fortress."

"Does that mean I won't be able to wait for her?"

He shook his head. "I thought you knew," he apologized. "We'll wait in the SUV or on the sidewalk. She'll walk out to us."

"Are there going to be cops there? Guards, I mean?"

He shrugged. "Maybe? I've never seen them there when

I've picked up one of the guys."

"But, they might be there today to intimidate her?"

He nodded. "They might."

Noting the strange tone of his voice, I asked, "What?"

He scratched his jaw as he yielded at a stop sign and said, "What if we're focusing on the jail when we should be focusing on something she saw before she was arrested? Back when she was a full-blown addict?"

"But you said that you that you looked into everything before we got married," I reminded him. "You paid her drug debts and Andrei's. You said there was nothing else out there that could hurt us."

"I could have been wrong. I could have missed something. Or maybe someone held onto her debt to use against her later."

"Like blackmail?"

"Yes."

I considered that for a moment. "If we are wrong and the parking lot mess and the voicemail are from before she went to jail, it could be anyone."

"Did Teague use drugs? Maybe he and Ruby crossed paths when she was struggling. Maybe that's how he knows what was said to you when you were attacked."

"He never used when we were together. What he's been doing since then?" I shrugged. "I suppose anything is possible."

As we waited to make a left turn behind a long line of cars, he made a frustrated sound and tapped his fingers on the steering wheel. "I shouldn't be stressing you out with what-ifs. Once Ruby is safe at the house, we can question her and get the answers we need."

"You're not stressing me out." I reached over and placed my hand on his thigh. "And, maybe, we just ask her. Not question. That sounds very police-like. If we try to interrogate her, she's going to get defensive."

He grunted but nodded. "Fine."

Hoping that things would go well between Ruby and Ivan, I kept my hand on his thigh while he drove downtown. I scrolled through my phone with the other hand, hastily typing replies to my friends. Wondering if Lena had the updated contact info for our mutual friend who worked at Teague's firm, I asked, "What time is it in Russia?"

"Which part?" When he saw the face I was making, he laughed. "I'm serious!" He glanced at the dashboard clock. "It's 8 p.m. in Novosibirsk. It's 10 p.m. in Yakutsk. Way out on the coast, near Alaska, it's after one in the morning."

"Moscow," I clarified. "Where one of your best friends lives."

"It's after 4." He glanced at me with one of his amused grins. "In the afternoon."

While I typed a message to Lena and apologized if I bothered her while she was napping off her jetlag, I asked, "How do you even remember all of those time zones?"

He shrugged. "The same way you know what time it is in LA or NY. It's something I learned as a kid."

"Have you ever been to those places?" I put my phone in the cup holder and focused my attention on him. "Novo-brisk?"

His mouth twitched. "Novo-SI-birsk," he corrected gently. "Once. We had a friend who hooked us up with stolen train tickets. We traveled all over that summer." He smiled at what was probably one of his better childhood memories. "There's a zoo there. In Novosibirsk," he explained. "You would like it."

"Maybe you can take me someday. Our kids, too," I added with a hopeful smile.

"Someday," he replied, covering my hand with his for a moment. "But it will have to be a summer trip. Our kids won't know how to handle the cold after growing up in this humidity and heat."

"It's cold right now." I gestured to the overcast skies.

He snorted. "This isn't cold."

I rolled my eyes. "Oh, here we go." Imitating his voice, I said, "I am strong as a polar bear. I swam in frozen lakes and played naked in the snow when I was four!"

"I don't sound like that," he protested. "And I never swam in a frozen lake."

"But you played naked in the snow?"

"Probably," he admitted. "The home I lived at around that age wasn't very attentive. We ran wild."

He didn't like talking about his childhood, and I hated that I had brought up some ugly memories. "I'm sorry, Ivy. I didn't mean to bring that up."

"Don't be sorry. It's fine." He glanced at me and smiled. "If our kids are anything like me, we're going to be exhausted by the end of the day. I was a little maniac, climbing, and jumping and digging and destroying everything in my way."

"I can see that." It wasn't hard to imagine a tinier version of him running around, causing mayhem on a playground. "Ruby was always a risk-taker, too."

"I bet you followed all the rules and were your teacher's

favorite student."

I bristled at his guess but had to admit he was right. "Yes. Most of the time."

"Well, let's hope our kids take after you more than me."

"No way! There is so much about you that I want our kids to inherit."

"Like?"

"Your tenacity. Your loyalty. Your generosity. The way you love me," I added, thinking of how completely he had committed himself to me.

He seemed a little embarrassed by my praise and cleared his throat. "I…thank you." He glanced over and caught my gaze. "I appreciate that you feel that way."

Pleased with his gratitude and acceptance of a compliment, I leaned over and lifted up out of my seat to quickly kiss his cheek. "You're welcome."

"Sit back," he scolded with a rumbling laugh. "We're in morning traffic with all of these crazy drivers."

He had a point so I made a show of sitting primly in my seat. "Speaking of cars and drivers…"

"Yes?"

"I was thinking about taking Ruby with me to test drive some cars at Alexei's lot."

"I think that sounds like a good idea."

I narrowed my eyes at his too quick reply. "Really?"

"Yes. Really."

"Uh-huh."

"What?" He laughed and shook his head. "I'm being nice and agreeing that your sister deserves a nice afternoon with you, and now I'm suspicious?"

"I mean…"

"Erin." He looked over to make sure I understood he was serious. "I know you've missed your sister. I know you want to fix your relationship. *I* want *you* to have that with her. If that means you two go car shopping? Good."

There was no mistaking the truth reflected in his eyes. He really did want that for me. "Well, thank you."

He nodded. "You're welcome."

Teasingly, I said, "Look at us! Communicating like adults! Talking about our feelings!"

He snorted. "Don't expect it too often. I have a reputation to uphold."

"Yes, as my big, sweet, marshmallow."

He groaned. "I hope you don't say that to other people."

"Never," I answered hastily, hiding my smile.

"Erin!"

"What?"

"Nothing." He reached over and grabbed my hand, lifting it and noisily kissing the back of it. "I love you."

"Even if I go around telling everyone what a marshmallow you are?"

He grunted. "Even if you do that."

We drove the rest of the way in silence, me smiling, and him still holding my hand. As he navigated the busy streets, I tried to control my expectations for the day. I had to be mindful of everything Ruby had endured. She had gone from a raging addict to clean and sober and not fully by her choice. She had lost the man she loved and her freedom. She had gone through God only knew what behind bars. When she came out of that inmate processing center, she wasn't going to be the sister I had known all my life. She was going to be different, probably harder and more mistrusting, and I had to give her grace.

Ivan's description of the building was correct. It was ugly and very plain. Across the street, there was a tall building made of wheat-colored stone. "What is that?"

"Court," he said, pulling into a public parking lot right next to the building. He took his wallet from the center console and plucked a ten from it. He rolled down the window and handed it to the bored-looking attendant. "Keep the change."

"Thanks, man."

"Where do you want to park?" he asked while his window finished rising. There were dozens of empty spaces this early in the morning, so we had our pick.

"How about this first row? Next to the building? She'll see us when she comes out, right?"

"I think so." He chose a spot in that row and parked. "Now, we wait."

"I'm not good at waiting."

"I know you aren't." He brushed his fingers along my jaw. "But you've waited all these months to get her out, so what's a few more minutes?"

"I guess when you put it like that…"

As if on cue, I spotted the familiar form of my sister rounding the corner. I unlatched my belt and practically tumbled out of the front seat before bounding toward her like an overwhelmed child. She stiffened when she saw me running, probably instinct after being incarcerated and on edge all the time, but relaxed when she realized it was me. "Ruby!"

"Jesus, Erin!" she exclaimed with a laugh of disbelief as I launched myself at her. "We saw each other a week ago!"

"It's not the same!" I hugged her tightly, not wanting to let go. It wasn't until that moment, feeling my sister's arms around me that I understood how much I had missed her. From the moment she fell into her drug habit, she had been lost to me, flitting in and out of my life when she needed something. At least, when she was in jail, I didn't have to worry about where she was sleeping or if she was eating or even alive. I had been able to let that anxiety go, but I had replaced it with the worry about what was happening to her on the inside. Was she being hurt? Harassed? Bullied? Beaten? It was awful not to know, to lurch from one phone call to one visit to one phone call on a never-ending cycle of intermittent contact.

But she was out now. She was coming home. I had already lost my parents, and I swore right then, as I refused to let go of my embrace, that I wasn't going to lose my sister, too.

CHAPTER NINE

"**S**O, DO YOU want to go straight home or stop for breakfast somewhere?" I knelt in my seat, facing her in the middle row as she slipped into the hoodie from the bag I had prepared. "Ivan and I have the day off, so we can do whatever you need to do."

Ruby made a face. "You didn't both need to take the day off."

"I needed a driver," I explained.

"Why?" she asked, frowning.

"Why do you think?" Ivan asked, skipping straight over the niceties.

I cringed, and Ruby looked at me with confusion. "What the hell does that mean?"

"Ivan," I pleaded quietly. "We talked about this."

He clenched his jaw and turned his gaze toward his window. "I'm sorry."

"No, no, no," Ruby interjected, sitting forward and aggressively grabbing the sleeve of his jacket. She jerked hard enough to make him sway and demanded, "If you have something to say to me, be a man and say it."

"Ruby!" Shocked at her behavior, I reached for her arm, and she suddenly balled up her fist as if to strike me.

"Don't. You. Dare," Ivan growled menacingly. "You touch your sister, and you'll be living under a fucking bridge for all I care."

"Ivan," I whispered harshly. "Please."

His jaw remained tight as he met my pleading gaze. "I'm serious, Erin. If she hits you, that's it."

"I know." I placed a soothing hand on his shoulder and turned to face my sister. She seemed just as surprised by her behavior as I was. She had dropped her hands and looked dazed. Hating that she felt so out of place and so on edge after her time inside, I carefully took her hand. "Ruby, I'm sorry. I shouldn't have grabbed you like that."

From the corner of my eye, I could see Ivan staring with disbelief. I could practically hear him asking what the hell I was doing apologizing for almost being struck by my sister.

"No." Ruby lowered her gaze and shook her head. "I'm sorry. I'm just…it's reflex now." She swallowed hard. "It was hard the last few weeks, and I haven't been getting much sleep."

"It's okay," I assured her. "Really. I know this is going to be hard for you to adjust to everything." Chancing a glance at Ivan, I silently begged him to let it go. He nodded stiffly and turned his attention back to the windshield. Giving Ruby's hand a gentle squeeze, I said, "Maybe we should have a hands-off rule for a bit?"

She nodded. "Yeah. That's…yeah."

"Okay. Good." I let go of her hand, and she settled back into her seat and buckled her belt. With Ivan's blundering accusation, there was no point in waiting to ask her until later. "So, the thing is," I started carefully, "last week, I was leaving my barre class, and, well, I was robbed."

"Attacked," Ivan corrected gruffly. "She was attacked by men with ski masks. They robbed her and set her car on fire."

Ruby's face slackened with shock and horror. "What? Why? Who?"

"You really don't know?" Ivan watched her in the rearview mirror and seemed convinced by her reaction.

"Of course, I don't know who attacked my sister!" she snapped angrily. "I know I'm a fuck up, but I wouldn't stand by and let that happen."

"I know you wouldn't," I hurriedly assured her. "It's just that…well…"

"What?" she demanded. "What is it?"

Holding her gaze, I explained, "The guy who had me shoved against a car told me that if you didn't keep your mouth shut, they would be back for both of us."

There was a flicker of understanding in her face, so quick and faint that I thought I had imagined it. Before I could ask if she knew what he meant, Ruby said, "I have no idea what that means. I don't know anything that could get anyone hurt."

"If you're lying," Ivan cut in, "you're risking your safety and your sister's."

"Obviously," she replied. "I'm not lying. I don't know what those men want me to stay quiet about, Erin."

You're lying. I wanted to shout at her, to demand she tell me the truth, but I knew her too well for that. She would clam up and grow obstinate. Instead, I calmly nodded. "I believe you, Ruby. I know you wouldn't lie about something so serious. Something that could get us both killed."

"I wouldn't," she insisted, brazenly lying to my face. Then, with a nasty look, she glanced at Ivan. "If anyone has a reason to hurt you, it's because of him."

Before Ivan could turn in his seat to tell her off, I placed a calming hand on his arm and pinned her in place with a stern glare. "Ruby, don't even try it. We aren't your enemies, and you're not going to turn us against each other. We're all family, and we're all in this together."

She rolled her eyes. "Yeah. Whatever."

Feeling the aggravation pulsing off of Ivan in waves, I turned in my seat and let my hand slide down his arm to his hand. He instantly curled his fingers around mine, showing me that we were okay and would talk about this whole mess later. He lifted my hand and kissed the back of it, drawing a disgusted noise from Ruby in the backseat.

Anxiety started to build low in my stomach, swirling like a knot of snakes. Nauseated and on the verge of tears as my hopes for the day were dashed within minutes, I nevertheless put a smile on my face and asked, "Would you like to grab breakfast before we head home? Or maybe stop at Target or some other place you need to visit?"

"When do you meet your PO?" Ivan asked, crashing like a runaway car into my desperate attempt to get the day back on track. "Is it walk-in for the first visit or an appointment?"

"Appointment," Ruby said before tearing into the Pop-Tart foil with her teeth. "I want to go home. I need a shower and a nap."

Deflated, I kept my smile in place and nodded. "Okay. Home it is."

Ivan tried to keep hold of my hand as he backed out of our parking space, but I tugged it free and interlocked my fingers on my lap. My worst fears about our living situation were coming true. Ivan and Ruby disliked each other so much they were going to fight nonstop. Imagining months of them at each other's throats made me sick. The damage their inability to get along would inflict on our marriage, and my relationship with my sister was nothing to the risk of her relapsing and using drugs again to deal with the stress.

The tension in the SUV was unbearable. When we finally parked in our garage, I bailed first, unable to spend another moment with the two of them. Ruby followed, and Ivan trailed her. In the kitchen, it all came to a head before I could even try to avert the impending disaster.

"Let's just cut the shit," Ivan announced, slashing his hand through the air. Ruby crossed her arms, ready for the fight that was coming, and I held my breath and waited for the fireworks. "You're a guest in our house. We don't expect you to pay rent. We don't expect you to buy your own groceries or other necessities. What we do expect is that you keep your room clean, get a job and go to all of your probation appointments and classes. If you fuck around and get in trouble, you're out of here. If you do something that puts Erin in danger, you're out of here. If you keep up the attitude, you're out of here."

Ruby looked at me in disbelief. "Is he always a controlling asshole like this?"

"Ruby!"

"If you don't like the rules at my house—"

"Your house?" Ruby interrupted. "I thought this was Erin's house, too."

"Stop!" I stepped between them like a referee, my arms out

wide to keep them separated. "Ivan, stop antagonizing her." He frowned but didn't say anything in protest. Turning toward Ruby, I said, "Let me show to your room. You can get that shower and nap you wanted."

I didn't stick around to see if she made a childish face at him. I pivoted on my heel and marched from the kitchen, trusting that she would follow. She caught up to me in the formal dining room, and I quickly pointed out the other rooms on the main floor as we made our way to the staircase. She walked next to me as we climbed the stairs to the second floor and seemed to be surprised by the size of the house. We had grown up as upper-middle class, and our parents had done very well for themselves, but they had never lived as large as Ivan preferred. He worked so hard for his money, and after studying his—our—finances, it was clear that we could afford the level of lifestyle he wanted for us.

"So, we are on the other side of the hall," I gestured toward the master suite. "I put you here, so you have more privacy. The windows look out over the backyard. It's a very calming view."

I pushed the door to her room open and stood aside so she could enter first. She walked to the center of the room and turned in a slow circle as she studied the space. She gave in to her curiosity and checked out the closet and bathroom. Wanting her to feel welcome and comfortable, I said, "I kept the décor simple so you can add or change things. I brought your things from the apartment. Some of them are hanging in the closet or are on the bookshelves. There's a storage container in the closet with things for you to sort out when you're ready."

When she didn't say anything, I nervously added, "We can go shopping later to get anything you need."

"Why? So, you can rub all your money in my face?"

Whatever response I had been expecting from her, it wasn't this. "What do you mean?"

She rolled her eyes. "Come on, Ruby. Don't act so innocent. You know what I mean. You have all this." She threw her arms out wide. "And I have nothing."

"That's not true. You have your trust fund coming when you turn thirty, just like me."

Ignoring that fact, she barreled on, unleashing her frustrations on me. "I have to admit I'm really surprised at you, Erin. I thought you were the kind of girl who wanted to make her own way in life. Remember how you used to talk about going to college, buying your own house and your own car, and making your own way? Look at you now."

"What about me now?"

She gestured toward me. "Designer clothes. Designer purse. Designer shoes. Diamonds and gold. Living in this obscene fucking mansion all alone with your husband."

"Our home isn't obscene."

"*His* home, you mean," she corrected, cruelly pointing out Ivan's words from earlier. "You know, all this time I thought you were so boring and simple. You were just this annoying good girl who did everything Mom and Dad wanted. Who would have believed that you were just a gold digger in training the whole time?" With a curl of her lip, she asked, "What's your secret, little sister? Huh? How do you get a man as rich as Ivan to keep someone like you? Are you that good at sucking cock or do you have some kind of magic pussy that he can't get—"

"I'm not listening to this!" I cut her off angrily. Mouth dry, head pounding, I turned and headed for the door. I spun back toward her. "When you're ready to act like my sister—"

Ruby slammed the door in front of my face, ending our conversation on an ugly note. Reeling from the horrible shit she had said to me, I walked downstairs on shaky legs. My decision to bring her home with us seemed so stupid now. I should have known I was inviting trouble into my life and my marriage.

She's my sister. I have to help her.

But not at the cost of my marriage.

Rubbing my face, I returned to the kitchen, ready to speak to Ivan about the awful turn our morning had taken. Everything we had discussed about Ruby's first few days with us had gone out the window the moment he accused her of knowing about the parking lot attack. Why the hell hadn't he just kept his mouth shut?

"Ivan?" I called out as I entered the kitchen. Not seeing him there, I left the kitchen and made my way to his office, ducking into other rooms and spaces on the way to make sure he wasn't in them. When his office was empty, I searched our home gym, but he wasn't there either. A sinking feeling invaded the pit of my stomach, and I walked to the garage to confirm my suspicion.

His SUV was gone.

He was gone.

Numb and feeling so painfully alone, I wandered through the house until I reached the bottom of the staircase. My legs finally buckled, and I plopped down on the first step. I didn't even try to hold back my tears. Ruby's voice echoed in my head. She was right. I used to have so many ideas and plans for my future.

But then I met Ivan, and everything felt so perfect and natural, and my plans changed. I enjoyed working with him, and I was proud of all that I had accomplished at the Warehouse to grow the business. I was proud of the way I had taken control of his investment portfolio to diversify and adjust his riskier holdings to more stable earners that would protect us financially. I was proud of the house I had decorated and turned into a warm, inviting home and a place of respite for us. I was proud of our life.

So why did Ruby's ugly words make me feel so bad?

CHAPTER TEN

AGGRAVATED WITH THE way the morning had gone to shit, Ivan waited in line at Erin's favorite spot for breakfast tacos. The least he could do was bring home something she enjoyed so she could have a full belly when she ripped into him for being a complete asshole.

Why didn't you just keep your fucking mouth shut?

Pondering on that, he surveyed the area from the back of the line. The Jimenez sisters' brightly painted truck was always parked in the Warehouse parking lot on Fridays, and Erin was always one of the first in line to get her taco and Mexican hot chocolate fix. This morning, he'd tracked them down using Instagram and found them in an empty lot surrounded by construction and demolition. The sisters had a knack for finding the best place to park to feed a steady stream of hungry workers.

His phone started to vibrate in his back pocket. He tugged it free and glanced at the screen, expecting to see Erin calling, but it was Dimitri. "Dima?"

"Are you busy?" his friend asked.

"No," he answered, slipping easily into Russian.

"Listen, I had a chance to talk with that connection I mentioned the other day."

"And?"

"And she isn't interested in talking to us about her time working in corrections."

Shit. Her hesitation wasn't a good sign.

"Is there anything I can do to persuade her to talk to us? Or to Erin? Money?"

"No, she was very clear that she never wants to be asked about that period of her life ever again, and I agreed to let it go and never bring it up again."

He sighed. "I understand."

"I'm sorry, Vanya."

"It's fine. Thank you for trying."

"Of course." A baby shouted with frustration in the background, and Dimitri laughed. "I have to go. Sophia is demanding I pick her up and fly her around the house like an airplane."

Ivan laughed. "You better go then."

After the call ended, he slipped his phone back into his pocket and wondered where he could go for answers. He was sorely tempted to break Nikolai's order to leave Kostya alone. The cleaner was rumored to be back in town, hiding out with Holly Phillips, of all people. There was a story there, some kind of secret that Nikolai was hiding, about Holly. He had his own suspicions, but he didn't dare ask. When Nikolai was ready for people to know Holly's story, he would tell them.

"Hey, Judy, look! El Ruso found us way over here on the other side of Houston!" Angie Jimenez, the younger of the two sisters, leaned forward on her elbows at the ordering window and smiled at him. She stuck her head out the window and looked around as if trying to find Erin. "Where's your wife?"

"Home."

"Uh-huh," Angie said, clearly believing there was more to the story. She grabbed her pad of tickets and a pencil. "The usual?"

"Yes."

As she scribbled on the pad, she called out, "Two barbacoa! Two chorizo, potato and egg! One bean and cheese. Large hot chocolate. Bottle of OJ. Extra pico in the bag."

"Add two bacon, egg, and cheese," he instructed, thinking that was the safest option for Ruby. "And another hot chocolate."

Angie yelled out the additions and then ripped the ticket free. She thrust it at him. "Tell Erin I have a new hot chocolate recipe I want her to test on Friday."

"Thanks. I will." He moved down to the window to pay and then waited nearby for his name to be called. Thoughts of Kostya and Nikolai circled round in his head. Faced with the choice between pissing off Nikolai or getting help to keep Erin and Ruby safe, he chose the latter. Nikolai would forgive him. Eventually, he would understand why Ivan had done it.

He called the most recent number he had for the cleaner, not at all surprised when it redirected to a voicemail box. "It's Vanya. Call me."

"El Ruso!" The cashier called out the nickname the sisters had given him and plunked his order down at the window.

He grabbed the paper bag and drink carrier and made his way back to his SUV. His phone started to buzz in his pocket, and he bit the paper bag to free his hand to open the door and then retrieve it. He dropped the bag onto his seat and answered. "Hello?"

"I can't believe it's taken you this long to call me," Kostya greeted with amusement in his raspy voice.

"I was told you're on vacation or maybe retired." He shifted the food and drinks into the passenger seat and climbed into the SUV.

"Fucking Nikolai," Kostya growled. "He's not my mother. He doesn't get to decide what I do."

"Does Holly?" Ivan dared to ask.

Kostya went silent. After a long moment, he admitted, "Yes."

"Welcome to the club," he grunted and punched the ignition button. "Listen, you know why I'm calling, yes?"

"Parking lot attack. Ex-con sister. Ex-boyfriend in money trouble. Lone Star Hitler," he listed off all the problems in Ivan's life. "Do you want me to handle it?"

Ivan frowned. "No, I don't want you to *handle* anyone."

"Fine." Kostya sounded almost glum. "I suppose you want me to dig around and see what I find?"

"Yes."

"I can put some of my spiders on Erin, if you like," Kostya offered. "They're very discreet but also very deadly if the situation calls for it."

Erin would be angry once she realized she was being followed, but he couldn't risk anything happening to her. "Discreet is good."

"Do you want me to tap her phone and email?"

"No." Keeping her safe was one thing. Invading her privacy was another.

"GPS on her phone and vehicle?"

"Yes, but she hasn't chosen a replacement car yet."

"Is she going to Alexei?"

"Yes."

"I've got it covered." Kostya seemed to be running through a checklist. "Does she have a favorite handbag? A pair sunglasses? Something she carries every day?"

"She has dozens of both and changes them all the time. You can't track her that way."

"Phone it is," Kostya muttered. "What about the sister? You want the same on her?"

"Yes." He hesitated. "Something happened inside the jail. I think it was something bad. Something very bad."

"There are rumors," Kostya admitted. "One of my spiders heard them a few months ago, but they weren't able to find any proof."

"Rumors of?"

"Sex trafficking."

"Inside the jail?"

"Yes. It happens all the time. If you spend any time on the darker parts of the internet, you'll find all kinds of shit filmed inside prisons. High paying clientele will order certain types of scenes or acts. It's good money for the distributors and producers," he explained with disgust in his voice.

"There was a voicemail on the night of that charity party," Ivan said, unable to forget the horrible screams. "There was a woman. Latina. Not Mexican. She sounded Honduran, maybe."

"You always did have an ear for accents," Kostya remarked. "What was she saying in the voicemail?"

"She was screaming. She was being beaten."

"A warning to Erin," Kostya guessed. "Or to the sister," he

amended. "She may have seen something while she was doing her time." He hesitated. "Or she's on one of those tapes."

Ivan clenched the wheel as rage overwhelmed him. If that were true, if Ruby had been abused in jail, Erin would never forgive herself for letting her sister go to jail to learn her lesson. "If Ruby was abused, you know I'll have—"

"I know," Kostya cut him off. "I know. If it comes to that, I don't have a problem making it happen."

That was the good thing about working with Kostya. He didn't blink at the prospect of even the most illegal acts.

"I'm going to text you a number. Use it to contact me. I'll be in touch."

The call ended, and he dropped his phone into the cup holder. When he reached over to adjust the drink carrier to make sure it wouldn't tip while he drove, he spotted Erin's hot pink phone on the floorboard. Feeling like a serious asshole, he picked it up and moved it to a cup holder. He had left without a word and had unknowingly taken her phone, cutting of the easiest way for her to contact him. He hastily buckled his belt and reversed out of his spot, all the while wondering how mad she was going to be when he returned. Even walking into the house with tacos in hand might not be enough to soothe her. If he didn't end up with a cup of hot chocolate dumped on his head, he would consider it a win.

He pulled into the garage and didn't waste any time grabbing the food, drinks, and her phone. Ready to face his wife and apologize, he entered the house through the mudroom and made his way to the kitchen. He stopped in the arched doorway at the sight of a red-eyed and sniffling Erin standing at the marble island and eating handfuls of sugary cereal straight from the box. She stuffed her hand back into the box and then froze, finally noticing him in the doorway.

Lamely, he lifted the paper bag and drink carrier. "I went for tacos and hot chocolate."

Her lower lip wobbled as she set aside the box. "You left without saying anything."

"I know. Fuck. I'm sorry." He crossed the space between them and placed the bag and drink holder on the countertop. He slid his arms around her and tugged her in for a hug. Pressing his lips to the top of her head and then her cheek, he repeated, "I'm sorry. I felt so stupid for fucking up, and I wanted to do something that would make it even a little better. I thought breakfast would help."

"It does," she sniffled against his chest. "But I'm still mad about the way you acted in the parking lot!"

"I know. I deserve it." He closed his eyes and breathed in the familiar scent of her shampoo. "I don't know why I acted like that. I've been worrying about who hurt you for days, and she was sitting back there, acting as if she had no idea what you had been through, and I lost it."

"You have to try harder, Ivan," she urged, leaning back to stare up at him. Her beautiful eyes silently pleaded with him. "You have to try not to antagonize her. She knows how to push your buttons. Until she realizes we aren't trying to control or lie or betray her, she's going to be difficult. You're an adult. You can control your own behavior."

Duly chastised, he nodded. "I know. I'll try. I will." As he released Erin, he said, "I'll go apologize to your sister."

"She may not answer the door. She was…," Erin paused as if searching for the correct word, "testy earlier."

He had a feeling there was much more to that story. Guilt gripped him at the idea of Erin being here alone while her sister lashed her with whatever spiteful nonsense she decided to spew at that moment. He plucked two of the burritos and the second hot chocolate from the bag and carrier. "I'll be back in a few minutes. You should eat some real food." He eyed the box of carb-heavy cereal with disdain. "That shit is going to give you diabetes."

"And these tacos are going to clog my arteries with all the delightfully fat goodness wrapped up in them," she replied before snatching up her drink and the bag of tacos and retreating to the breakfast nook.

As he climbed the stairs, he considered that not so long ago, he didn't even know what the hell a breakfast nook was. Or a gallery wall, he thought as his gaze moved to the artfully arranged photos and paintings on either side of the wide staircase. He hadn't ever given much thought to color palettes or things like modern farmhouse or industrial chic until Erin had moved in and started showing him things she had pinned on Pinterest or screenshotted on Instagram. She had lured him into watching shows like *Fixer Upper* and convinced him to take her to Round Top where he happily followed her around while she plucked furniture and décor from vendor stalls. He hadn't even minded the small fortune he had spent in shipping for the things that wouldn't fit in the SUV.

He liked the way she had transformed his house into an actual home. He didn't much care about the colors on the walls or the pillows on the couches or the patterns on the rugs. What he did care about was the way he felt when he walked through the house. He hadn't ever felt as comfortable and at ease as he did these days, surrounded by all the thoughtfully chosen pieces Erin had purchased and arranged for their home. He could feel her love for him and her excitement for their future and their life together in every little thing she had done.

Outside Ruby's door, he sighed. This was either going to end with a truce or a shouting match. Hoping for the truce, he knocked loudly on the door and stepped back, making sure to give her plenty of room. The door swung open to reveal Ruby with wet hair and different clothes, things he recognized from one of Erin's shopping trips. Scowling, she asked, "What the hell do you want?"

He had to bite back the urge to tell her off. Instead, he held out the breakfast he had gotten for her. "It's from Erin's favorite taco truck. I figured you were hungry for something that doesn't have powdered eggs and fake bacon in it."

She eyed the food with distrust. "How do I know it's not soaked in polonium?"

"Seriously? Do you think I'm going to poison you? If I wanted to get rid of you, Ruby, I would have done it while you were in jail, and I had plenty of cover." He thrust the food at her. "Take it. Eat it. Throw it in the trash. I don't care."

She snatched the food from him. "Fine. Whatever."

He put his hand on the door to keep her from slamming it in his face. "No, not yet." He kept the door open. "Your sister has done more than you can ever imagine to make things better for you. She went to that pigsty apartment you left behind and sorted through all of that rotting food and trash and the piles of filthy, moldy clothes to find things to salvage for you. She paid for the broken lease, the back rent, and the damage with her own money. She's been using her salary draw from the gym to cover your attorney fees, the repairs on the house you trashed, and your restitution because she didn't want you to be saddled with the full amount when you got out."

She seemed startled by that information, but he wasn't ready to stop yet.

"She's been going to counseling to learn how to help you adjust and be successful. She has a stack of books next to the bed that she's been reading and studying because she wants to do everything right." He pushed the door open enough to point at the green binder on the small coffee table by the reading chair Erin had chosen. "She spent days on that, putting together all the information you'll need to make this second part of your life work. So, maybe, you could show a little fucking appreciation for what she's done." He breathed out heavily. "She loves you. You're her sister. You're her family. She believes in you the same way she believes in me. If you let her support you, there's nothing you can't accomplish, but if you fight her every step of the way, you'll end up right back where you started."

Ruby swallowed hard and finally nodded. "Yeah," she said softly. "Okay."

Glad that was done, he gestured to the nightstand. "I left you some things you'll need in that top drawer. The cash is yours to cover your expenses until you find a job. The noise-canceling headphones should be self-explanatory."

When understanding hit, she made a face. "Gross!"

"At least, I warned you." He backed away from the door and started back toward the staircase. Ruby shut the door behind him. The fact that she didn't slam it surprised him.

Downstairs, he found Erin scrolling her phone and nibbling on one of her tacos piled high with pico de gallo. He didn't know how she could stand eating something so spicy and never get heartburn. Taking the seat next to her, he grabbed one of his breakfast tacos and peeled away the aluminum.

"Everything okay?" she asked guardedly as he took his first bite. He nodded as he chewed, and she visibly relaxed. "Good."

His phone vibrated in his back pocket, and he shifted on his chair to retrieve it. He glanced at the screen and frowned. "It's Paco."

"You better answer it. He wouldn't call on your day off unless all hell was breaking loose at the gym."

Agreeing with her, he swept his finger across the screen. "Paco?" he answered gruffly.

"Boss, I know you're on your day off, but we have a problem with the heat," Paco rushed out in lightning-fast Spanish. "I called the company that did the installation and service, but they can't get anyone here until tomorrow. We tried turning the system off, but it's still blowing hot air. It's ninety-fucking-degrees in here."

"Shut down the gym and send everyone home if you think that's best," Ivan suggested. "I'll be there as soon as I can."

"What's wrong?" Erin asked in between sips of hot chocolate.

"Heating system at the gym," he grumbled and shoved the rest of his taco in his mouth.

"You're going to choke eating like that," she warned with a shake of her head. "And, not to be that kind of wife, but I did tell you that the HVAC system was acting strange back in November and you said—"

He groaned. "I know. I know."

"Well, as long as you know."

"I'm sorry I have to bail on our day off," he apologized as he gathered up the rest of his breakfast and his orange juice.

"Don't worry about it," she urged. "This is the reality of owning a business."

"Will you be okay?" He glanced toward the ceiling. "If she starts her shit with you…"

"I'll handle it," she assured him. "But, I don't think she will. She needs time to decompress. I'm not going to bother her. She can find me when she's ready."

"That's a good idea. Give her some space."

"Will you be home for dinner?" she asked as he stood and tucked his phone into his pocket.

"Maybe? I'll keep you updated."

"The info for our HVAC service contract is in the red binder on the shelves behind my desk. The copy of our contract with the fee schedule is behind the HVAC tab with the rest of the PM records. There's also a couple of flyers we've gotten from other companies that want our business. If you feel like we need to change providers, there are options."

Amused by her perfectly organized system, he leaned down and kissed her. "I'll make this up to you."

"You don't have to."

"I want to." He kissed her again. "*Ya tebya lyublyu.*"

"I love you, too."

Thoughts of how he would make it up to her rattled around in his head as he drove to the Warehouse. When he pulled into the parking lot, most of the fighters who trained daily as part of the gym's full-time professional roster were doing their workouts outside. He stopped a few times as he walked toward the entrance to correct forms or give coaching. Once he stepped inside the building, he grimaced. Paco wasn't exaggerating. It was as hot as a sauna in there.

He found his longtime co-trainer in the utility room at the rear of the warehouse, shouting all sorts of foul things at the heating system. He stepped up beside Paco and tried a few different things, but when none of them worked, he walked over to the electrical panel on the far wall and flipped the breaker for the HVAC, killing it for the moment. They tried to reset it, hoping that would fix the problem, but when that failed, he flipped the breaker again and made his way to the office he shared with Erin.

As he flipped through her neatly organized maintenance binder, Paco stopped in front of the wall-mounted monitors that were part of the gym's recently updated security system. He made a strange noise, and Ivan looked up from the binder to ask, "What's wrong?"

"This truck has been driving by the gym two or three times a day for at least a week." Paco pointed it out on the monitors. "This one. It's a late 90's Silverado. Tan. Gun rack."

Ivan moved closer and watched as Paco rewound the footage. Not wanting to jump to conclusions, he said, "It could be someone working nearby. Maybe on the apartments going up a few blocks down?"

"Maybe," Paco replied, sounding unconvinced. "Might be someone casing us for a robbery."

"They wouldn't get much," Ivan grunted. "Carrying out

the equipment would take hours, and we don't keep any cash on hand."

"Maybe they're looking for someone."

That suggestion caught his attention. Was it one of the men who had attacked Erin and Zoya? "Can you save that? Print out some copies and put them up in the locker room. Try to get the license plate if you can. Let's ask everyone to look out for it."

"Sure, boss."

While Paco handled that, Ivan called their HVAC contractor. Seven hours and thousands of dollars later, he had a new system scheduled to be installed the next day. When the technician pointed out that the problem with the old system could have been repaired when it first started showing issues, Ivan groaned inwardly. Erin would never let him forget this. She wouldn't bring it up in a malicious or cruel way. She would simply have to look at him, and he would know that she was thinking about the time she asked him to do something that he forgot to do and cost them an outrageous amount of money.

By the time he pulled into the garage, it was nearing eight. Erin had texted earlier, letting him know that dinner was in the refrigerator. She had been happy to report that Ruby had finally come out of her room and shared a meal with her. It seemed there were no small victories where her sister was concerned.

The house was quiet when he entered. Thinking about the truck driving by the gym, he walked the entire first floor, checking windows and doors and setting the alarm for the night. He had already sent a photo of the truck and the license plate information to Kostya. All he could do now was wait for some news on that end.

He quickly ate the dinner she had left for him and loaded his dishes into the dishwasher before heading upstairs. He went into the extra bedrooms upstairs, checking the locks on the windows. When he neared Ruby's room at the end of the hall, he noticed the door was cracked, and the lights were on. He lightly knocked on the door. "Ruby?"

"Yeah? What?" she called from inside the room.

"Can you check your windows? Make sure they're all locked?"

The door swung open suddenly. She stood there in a matching plaid flannel pajama set Erin had picked out and crossed her arms. "What's wrong?"

"Nothing," he assured her. "I like to make sure the house is locked down at night."

She narrowed her eyes. "Is there something you're not telling me?"

Thinking it was rich for her to ask that when she was probably lying about knowing what had happened to Erin, he turned it around on her. "Is there something you're not telling me? Maybe why you're supposed to keep your mouth shut?"

Her lips flattened into a grim line. "No, there's not."

With a sigh, he admitted, "Our security cameras at the gym caught a truck driving by multiple times a day for the last week. I'm concerned it might be someone doing surveillance on Erin—or you."

She swallowed and shook her head. "I don't know about anyone in a truck."

"I believe you," he said, sure that she didn't know of the

specific vehicles used by the people who wanted to keep her silent. "When you're ready to trust me, I can help you. We both know that I'm connected to people who can keep you safe. Who can keep your sister safe."

"Like they kept her safe when she was kidnapped on your front porch a few months ago?"

The statement stung, but it was a fair question. "One of those men almost died trying to keep Erin safe."

"Yeah, well, I don't want anyone to die for me." She closed the door without another word, leaving him standing there and wondering how the hell he was going to get through to her.

When he finally entered the master suite, he found Erin splayed out on the loveseat in the sitting area of their bedroom. Even though she had piles of pajamas, she wore one of his old, faded tees. Her ankles were crossed and resting on the other end of the couch, and she had one of her favorite reality shows on the TV over the fireplace. She smiled when she noticed him. "Hey!"

"Hey." He crossed the room and leaned down to kiss her. "Thanks for dinner."

"Of course." She gave the bottom of his shirt a little tug. "So? What was the damage to our business account?"

He grimaced. "We can talk about it in the morning."

She laughed. "That bad, huh?"

He sighed. "Go ahead and get it out."

"Nah, I'm saving this I-told-you-so for our next argument," she decided. "Just going to stow it away until it's useful."

"You are so mean," he said, leaning down to kiss her one

more time. "I'm going to shower."

He didn't waste time and went through his nightly routine in record time. He had other plans for tonight. Plans that didn't include mindless TV or discussing his fuck-up with the heating system at the gym.

He didn't even bother with clothes. As soon as he was dry and his teeth were brushed, he shut off the light and stalked across the bedroom to where Erin still lounged on the loveseat. She eyed him with an amused gleam, surely recognizing that he was in the mood for only one thing. He bent down and snatched her up off the loveseat, tossing her over his shoulder and giving her naked bottom a good smack.

"Ivan!" she squealed with laughter. "What are you doing?"

"Making it up to you, remember?" He set her down by the bed and yanked the tee up and over her head. He threw it aside, not caring where it fell. He took a moment to enjoy the sight of her naked body. She was so beautiful and sexy. He didn't think he would ever get tired of staring at her like this.

He picked her up again and deposited her in the middle of the bed before crawling over her. He grabbed both slim wrists in one hand and held them over her head. Capturing her mouth, he kissed her until she was panting and rubbing her thighs together beneath him. Still holding her wrists, he nipped and suckled his way down her body, making it all the way to her navel before traveling back to her mouth.

"Ivan," she sighed happily.

But he didn't want soft sighs and moans. He wanted her begging and screaming. He wanted her to go wild and use him for her own pleasure. He wanted to make her come so hard and so many times that she would drop limp and exhausted to the bed and sleep with a smile on her face.

Using his grappling skills, he flipped her on top of him while rolling onto his back. She giggled at the sudden movement and then gasped when he grabbed her thighs and hauled her higher up his body. He reached back to grab the pillow under his head and threw it across the room, hearing it hit the wall with a thump. Flat on his back, he was in a better position for what he wanted most—a taste of his wife.

"You don't have to make it up to me like this," Erin said, biting her lip as she stared down at him between her thighs. She shuddered when he kissed and nibbled the sensitive skin there. "I mean, you can if you want to…"

"I've been thinking about this since I left." He nuzzled closer to where he really wanted to be and slid his hands from her waist to her ass, lifting her up a little higher and pulling her right down onto his face.

"Wait!" She tried to squeeze her thighs shut, but he kept them open with his broad shoulders. "My sister can hear us!"

"Not for long," he said before swiping her cunt with his tongue. "I left a pair of noise cancelling headphones in her room."

"Thank god for technology," she whimpered and then relaxed. She placed her palms on the upholstered headboard for support and moaned as he licked up and down her slit. When he fluttered his tongue over her clit, she threw her head back and cried out, "Ivan!"

Grinning, he let his tongue make amends for all the stress and upset he had caused her that morning. He suckled and lapped, overcome with her taste and scent. Memories of the first time he went down on her, right here in this house, rushed to the forefront of his mind. He had always enjoyed giving a woman pleasure, but he had never initiated that early in a relationship. He hadn't even asked her out on a date before he had his face buried between her legs, learning all her secrets with his tongue.

Even then, that first night, he had known she was it. It was as if she had been made for him, as if he had been waiting all those years to find her. His strange and harsh life had brought him from Russia to Houston, putting him right in the middle of her life's journey. The way their lives had intersected couldn't possibly be chance. It was always meant to be.

"Ivan. Ivan. Ivan." Her thighs tensed, and she pressed down against his mouth, seeking his tongue with her movements. "Please. Oh, please, don't stop. Don't stop. Don't!"

She came with a strangled cry, and he held tight to her hip and ass, holding her right there on his face while he made her scream. Every time she tried to lift away, he tugged her back down, using his superior strength to force through the waves of her orgasm. She let go of the headboard, placing her hands on either side of his head, and whipped her hips back and forth on his mouth, going wild as a second and more intense climax overwhelmed her. He smacked her ass—hard—his palm bouncing from plump cheek to plump cheek. She cried out with a mix of joy and pain and then screamed his name.

Smiling against her inner thigh, he let her go, and she dramatically dropped off of him, landing in a heap as she panted to catch her breath. He didn't even get a chance to try to make another move before she surprised him by aggressively shoving him back onto the bed. She flipped back her hair and planted both hands on his chest before throwing her leg over his hips and straddling him. She reached down between them, gripping his aching cock in her soft hand, and stroked the length of him, squeezing as she reached the tip. He groaned and tried to shift her into position, but she wouldn't let him.

Instead, she began peppering kisses along his face and chest while stroking him slowly, just enough to keep him on edge. When she started to lick her way down his belly, he shuddered and clenched the sheets in both fists. She took her time, sliding lower and lower until her mouth hovered over his cock. With a wicked smile, she said, "My turn."

The second her lips wrapped around the head of his cock, he growled, "Fuck me."

She stopped sucking just long enough to promise, "That's the plan."

He threaded his fingers through her hair and lifted his head to watch as she drove him crazy with her tongue. She did follow through with her plan, eventually, but it was a long and very torturous time later.

CHAPTER ELEVEN

"**T**HIS PLACE IS outrageous," Ruby hissed as we toured the showroom floor of Alexei's flagship dealership the next morning. "Six figures for a car?"

"I know," I agreed, wincing at the sticker price on the sporty coupe in front of us. "It's a bit much."

"A bit?" she repeated sarcastically.

"Okay, a lot." My gaze drifted away from the showroom vehicles to the ones parked in neat rows outside. There were some late model midsize SUVs that caught my eye. Their prices seemed more palatable.

"Erin!" Alexei greeted as he drew near. "It's good to see you."

Smiling, I shook his head. "Good morning, Alexei."

"You know you outbid me on that basketball I wanted," he said. "I hope Vanya enjoys it."

"I'm sure he will. Speaking of bidding, how badly did Lena corrupt Shay?"

He laughed. "Not even enough to make me blink."

Noticing his glance toward Ruby, I introduced them. "Alexei, this is my sister, Ruby. Ruby, this is Alexei Sarnov. He's one of Ivan's oldest friends."

"Nice to meet you," he said, shaking her hand.

"Yeah," Ruby replied, her gaze lingering on his faded hand tattoos. "One of those friends, I see."

To his credit, Alexei took her remark in stride. "We've all made mistakes in our past."

"We sure have," she said, seemingly amused by his little dig.

"I see you two are looking at our latest models." He slipped right into car salesman mode. "Are you wanting to move up in vehicle? Vanya said you were in a smaller sedan. Are you thinking of staying in a similar class or would you like something with more room? A mid-size SUV maybe?"

"I want more space. I'm moving into a new phase of life, and I want to be ready for car seats and strollers." I felt a flutter of excitement at the idea of speaking my greatest desire into existence.

Alexei grinned. "You and Vanya will make a beautiful family together." He glanced around the showroom. "What about one of those?"

"It's nice," I said uncertainly. "Maybe slightly too expensive?"

"It might be," he agreed, "but I think you should get behind the wheel. A price is just a number until you get a feel for the way it drives."

Behind him, Ruby rolled her eyes, and I started to question my decision to bring her along on this trip. She schooled her face as Alexei turned toward her and said, "Why don't I grab some keys and you two can take it for a drive?"

"Sure. Sounds good," I answered, hoping he hadn't noticed Ruby's eyeroll.

"That Q8 is, like, ninety grand," Ruby whispered harshly

when he was out of earshot. "Are you seriously going to spend that kind of money on something that depreciates as soon as you roll off the lot?"

Instead of getting annoyed, I smiled. "You sound like Mom."

She reacted with surprise. "What?"

"Do you remember when Mom and Dad took us with them to buy a new car? You were, like, twelve? I was eight-ish."

"Like I could forget!" She laughed. "Mom had her calculator and red pen, and Dad droned on and on about depreciation and interest rates and APR until you fell asleep with that free ice cream cone melting all over your shirt."

I cringed. "I forgot all about the ice cream part."

"You smeared it all over their new seats on the ride home," she remembered with another gleeful laugh. "It was the one time I ever saw Dad that close to losing his patience."

"I never appreciated how calm they were," I admitted, allowing myself to feel a bit sentimental. "Now, I know better. They were really wonderful parents."

"They were," Ruby agreed without any of her usual sarcasm. After a moment, she confessed, "Sometimes, I wonder what they would think about us. About *me*."

Taking a step closer, I gently reached for her hand, giving her ample time to pull away if she wasn't comfortable. She let me take her hand in mine, and I said, "Ruby, they loved you. They would have moved heaven and earth to help you. They would have been so proud to see that you've taken responsibility, paid your dues, and are trying to put your life back together."

Sensing that she was a bit uncomfortable, I added, "But they probably wouldn't have like Ivan much."

She frowned. "You think? I mean—yes, the tattoos and the whole what-he-was-before thing—but he owns a successful business and loves you. I can't imagine they'd want more than that for you. Eventually, they would have learned to like him."

Hearing her praise Ivan stunned me. "Wait. When did you decide that you like Ivan?"

She rolled her eyes. "I *never* didn't like him."

"But you—"

"He was taking you away from me," she blurted out. "I was…" She glanced away briefly and sighed. "I was afraid, okay? I was so messed up on the drugs, and Andrei was dead. I was alone, and I was going to jail. Suddenly, this guy shows up, and you're obsessed with him. I was afraid you would forget me. I was afraid you would stop caring. I was afraid you would realize how awful I was and how much I had taken advantage of you and hurt you. He was going to steal you away, and I was going to be left behind."

"Ruby," I said, my heart aching for her. "It was never going to go that way. Never."

"I know." She squeezed my hand. "You came every single week to visit. You always answered my phone calls. You came back even when I was a complete bitch. You invited me to stay with you before I could even muster up the courage to ask. I never…I shouldn't have doubted you."

"It's okay. Really," I emphasized, seeing her eyes glistening with unshed tears. Unable to hold back, I wrapped my arms around her. If people were staring at us for hugging in the middle of a dealership, I didn't care. This was a discussion I had desperately wanted to have with my sister, and finally, it had happened. For the first time in years, I felt so much hope for our relationship as sisters.

When we separated, Alexei stood nearby, his gaze averted as he gave us some space. "If you're ready, we can go outside and pick one out for a test drive. I grabbed the keys for three different trims."

Outside in the chilly January morning, I chose the top of the line trim for my test drive. Alexei seemed happy with that choice and slid into the middle row of passenger seats for the drive. He didn't bother with high-pressure sales tactics. He let me enjoy the drive and ask questions that he easily answered, proving that he was a hands-on owner of his auto sales empire.

"Did you feel like this might be the one?" Alexei asked when we returned to the lot. "Or would you like to look at something else?"

"I like the size and the way it drives, but I'm not thrilled with the price," I said as I handed over the key fob. "That's not me trying to negotiate. That's me wondering if we could find something with a list price that's not so eye-watering."

He considered for a moment and then smiled. "I have something you'll like. It came in yesterday from my lot in Conroe." He led us toward a row of vehicles next to the rear of the building. "These haven't been put into our local system yet. That's why they're over here." He stopped in front of a shiny silver GLS. "It's two years old. One owner. Less than ten thousand miles. It basically sat in her temperature-controlled garage the whole time she owned it."

"Why?" I wondered as I opened the driver's side door for a better look.

"My GM told me she changed jobs after she bought the car and started working internationally. She decided to move overseas, and this was one of the last things she sold." He gestured for us to explore the vehicle. "I'll grab some keys, and you and your sister can take it around the block a few times."

"I like this one," Ruby announced after she hopped up into the passenger seat. "It feels a bit roomier." She turned in her seat to look at the middle row and cargo area. "You could probably fit two car seats in there comfortably. You wouldn't have to upgrade to a minivan until you have three kids."

I made a face at the idea of three little Ivans running wild in our home. "Let's just start with one."

She laughed. "Unless you end up with twins on your first go."

"I don't know if I'm ready to go from no kids to two at once." I couldn't even imagine the logistics of that. Two cribs, two car seats, double the bottles and diapers, and laundry and baths. "You'll have to stay with us forever."

She snorted. "Not a chance. I'm planning to be the aunt who fills them up with sugar and noisy toys and then drops them back off at your house."

"Wow. Thanks," I replied dryly. "So helpful."

"Here you go, Erin." Alexei returned with the key fob. "When you get back if you want to talk numbers, we can, or I can find something else for you to try."

We didn't need to try another vehicle. After the test drive, I decided I wanted it. The negotiation was painless and quick. The price he offered was fair according to what Ruby had found on the internet while we were on our test drive, and the discount on the warranty and service package I wanted made it a no-brainer. It was only when we got to the financing that we disagreed. Ivan had instructed Alexei to invoice him for the full price, but I wanted to finance it under my own name to continue building my credit profile. Another ten minutes of furiously texting back and forth with Ivan ended in me getting my way, much to Alexei's amusement.

"Thank you for bringing me," Ruby said a short time later as we left the dealership. "It was nice to do something normal."

"Is there anything else you'd like to do today? We can grab a late lunch after your appointment," I offered.

"Steak?" she asked hesitantly. "I can't remember the last time I ate a really good steak."

"Then we are definitely going to a steakhouse," I decided. "Any one in particular?"

As we debated where to get the best steaks in a not too crowded restaurant, I followed the navigation prompts on my phone. Next to me, Ruby radiated nervous energy. Even though she had served her time in prison, she had months and months of probation to finish. If she made any mistakes, they could send her back to jail.

"Do you want me to come inside with you?" I asked after I found a spot to park.

"I don't think they'll let you come into the meeting," she said, looking decidedly anxious.

"I don't mind sitting in the waiting room."

"No?"

"Nope."

When we entered the austere building, we were directed to a security checkpoint and then to the elevators. The entire building smelled stale and slightly sour. The lighting was poor, and the chairs in the waiting area outside the probation intake offices squeaked and wobbled precariously. While Ruby checked in for her appointment, I picked a few brochures off the end table next to my chair and skimmed through them.

"I wonder why they changed it from probation to community supervision?" I flashed the brochure at her as she took her seat.

"Someone probably did a study that said that it was better for an ex-con's self-esteem." She unlooped the elastic tie holding her auburn locks out of her face and then finger-combed her hair back before winding it into a loosely coiled bun. "There was a lot of that psychology bullshit inside."

"Was it helpful?"

She chortled. "Seriously?"

"Yes."

She shrugged. "I guess for some people it is."

"But it wasn't for you?"

"Not the way they wanted it to be," she replied cryptically.

Before I could ask her what she meant by that, her name was called. She picked up her scuffed leather purse, one of the few things I had managed to save from her apartment. "Wish me luck."

"Good luck, sis."

She smiled at that and left me behind in the waiting room. I couldn't help but marvel at the turn our relationship had taken. Maybe all she needed was a good night's rest in a safe place. Whatever the reason, I wasn't going to question it. As long as we were moving forward and growing closer, that's all that mattered.

Tucking the brochures into my purse, I pulled out my

phone and opened the texts from Ivan. He had sent me a mirror selfie, naked from the waist up, flexing his incredible muscles to apologize for our minor tiff over the vehicle financing. I sent back an invite for a work quickie later followed by a string of naughty emojis. He answered back quickly—he was on his lunch break—with his own emojis to confirm.

Hiding my smile and the flash of arousal that our messages caused, I swiped out of the message and noticed some texts farther down the list from a number I didn't recognize. Apprehensive after the unsettling voicemail I had received at the gala, I reluctantly opened the messages and was greeted with a chilling set of photos. Someone had been close enough to snap photos of Ruby and me at the dealership.

But it was the photo of me, sitting right where I was in that moment, that made my stomach churn with fear. I swallowed nervously and looked around the busy waiting room, half expecting to see masked men looking right back at me. My gaze lingered on the men waiting for their appointments. The ones who weren't white I disregarded immediately. There were seven who fit the description of the men from the parking lot attack, but I couldn't exactly march up to each of them and demand they show me their phone.

My gaze drifted to the hallway and the elevators. The man who took these photos could have already left. I hadn't been paying attention earlier, so it would have been easy to snap a quick photo and disappear. Or, maybe it wasn't a man. Maybe it was a woman.

Trying not to lose it, I pushed down the natural feelings of panic and tried to think logically. No one was going to try to hurt Ruby or me in the middle of a building teeming with cops and security guards. They might try to snatch us outside, but I was ready for that and would be paying attention. No, this was someone trying to get under my skin.

"You okay?" Ruby asked when she returned to my side.

"Look." I held out my phone, and she snatched it from my hand, scrolling through the photos and then glancing anxiously around the room.

"We need to get out of here." She thrust my phone back at me. "Text Ivan. Tell him we're coming to the gym. Forward those photos to him."

Relieved by her no-nonsense response, I followed her instructions and then matched her steps to the elevator. We got stepped into the car alone and rode down in tense silence. When we stepped out of the building, she asked, "Did Ivan text back yet?"

I checked my phone. "No, but the afternoon training block has already started. His phone is on his desk or got tossed to the side of the mats. He may not—"

I stopped mid-sentence when Ruby suddenly grasped my hand. I followed her gaze to the far end of the sidewalk, where a tall blond man leaned against the building. I couldn't see his eyes behind his aviator sunglasses, but there was something unnervingly familiar about him.

"Come on," Ruby urged and tugged my hand. "Get your keys."

While she hustled us across the street to the parking lot, I plucked my key fob from my purse and unlocked the doors when we were close. We hurriedly got into the SUV, and I locked the doors immediately, sealing us both inside where we would hopefully be safe. I started the engine, and without even waiting to fasten my seat belt, I pulled out of the parking space.

Ruby reached over and grabbed the seat belt from my right hand and snapped it into place. "Go!"

I rushed out of the parking lot as safely as I could and drove away from the probation office as we were being chased by the Devil himself. "Who was that?"

Ruby stopped chewing her thumb nail long enough to say, "A guard."

"I'm going to assume there's some sort of history with him?"

"Yes." She chewed her thumb nail again, a nervous habit she had had since we were kids. "It's complicated, and if I tell you everything, you're going to be in serious danger."

"I'm pretty sure I'm already in serious danger."

"Worse danger than you can imagine," she amended.

"I'm imagining the worst, Ruby." I glanced in the rearview mirror and noticed a truck that I had seen earlier that morning and then again in the parking lot of the probation office. "Do you see that tan truck a few cars behind us? It's an older model. Has a dented hood."

She twisted in her seat. "Yeah, I see it."

Before I could ask her to snap a photo, she used her new phone to take a few. "I think I got the plates."

"Is it him? The guard?"

"I can't tell." She studied her phone's screen. "Maybe?"

"What's his name? Was he one of your guards?" I glanced away from the road and noticed how upset she looked. My mouth went dry. "Did he hurt you?"

She worked up the courage to nod.

My breaths came faster as I realized that my sister had been abused. "Did he rape you?"

She nodded again. "Not just me."

"Is that what they want you to stay quiet about? The guards are abusing the prisoners?"

"That's part of it."

"There's more?" I exclaimed, sickened by the realization that my sister had been stuck in a horrific and traumatizing place for all those long months. "Ruby?"

She shook her head. "I can't, Erin. Not right now."

"Okay. It's fine. You don't have to say anything else until you're ready." I reached for her hand, and she interlaced our fingers, holding on for dear life. "Whenever you're ready, I'm here, and I'll listen."

"Thank you," she whispered, her hand shaking in mine. She glanced out the window and said, "You can tell Ivan, but no one else."

Ivan.

Once he found out what had happened, he would go ballistic. There would be no stopping his need for vengeance for his family. He would risk another prison sentence to make sure Ruby received the justice she deserved.

My thoughts turned from the shock of finding out my sister had been raped—probably more than once—by a prison guard to burning white-hot fury. I was overwhelmed by violent thoughts. I wanted to kill that piece of shit. I wanted to lock him in a cage with Ivan and let my husband teach that disgusting, worthless worm what real pain was.

For the first time in my life, I wanted to exploit all of

Ivan's connections. I wanted to do ugly, terrible things to the man who had hurt my sister. I wanted blood.

And, if I knew my husband, he would make sure I got it.

CHAPTER TWELVE

"THAT'S THE SEVENTH time you've checked your phone since you finished our paperwork," Ivan remarked as we waited to be called into our fertility appointment a few days later. He had his arm slung along the back of my chair, and soothingly rubbed my upper arm. "Ruby will be fine."

"How can you be sure?" She had stayed behind at the house while we attended our appointment, and even with the security system in place, I was nervous about her being alone after the unnerving run-in at the probation office. We hadn't seen or heard from Jodi Kavanaugh since that day, but I remained on edge, expecting him to jump out like the bogeyman where ever I went.

He shifted slightly and stroked my neck. "Kir and Stas are sitting at the house."

The two men trained at our gym but were also part of Nikolai's crew. "Why not hire one or two of Dimitri's guards?"

"Because they'll want to play by the book," he answered honestly.

"And Stas and Kir won't."

"Exactly."

Deciding this wasn't the place to discuss his reasons in-depth, I asked, "What are we going to do about Ruby finding a job? She can go a little while without one as long as she proves she's actively seeking work, but what if she can't get hired anywhere?"

Until my sister's experience, I had never given much thought to how felons found work after release. Seeing how many employers wouldn't even look at a felon's application, I suddenly had a better understanding of why so many offenders ended up back on drugs or in jail. Ruby was luckier than most. She had a safe place to stay, all the food she could ever want, and access to all the comforts and necessities of modern life. What about all the newly released prisoners who didn't have a support system like hers?

"I have an idea," Ivan said. "She'll probably hate it, but it's the best offer she's going to get."

Before I could ask about his idea, a nurse called us back for our appointment. My stomach fluttered with nervous energy, and I silently prayed this would be the start of a successful baby-making journey. With his hand on my lower back, Ivan walked beside me across the waiting room and down the hall lined with prettily framed photos of smiling parents and their babies. Instead of the expected exam room, we were taken to an office for our consultation, which helped me relax a little more.

Nancy, the patient education nurse, sat down with us and went over the process of working with the clinic. After briefly explaining the medical side of things, including some of the tests we would have and the options to achieve a healthy pregnancy, she said, "We have actual licensed therapists and counselors on staff if you would like to talk to someone as you go on this journey."

Ivan had draped his arm along the back of my chair again, and I could feel him tense at the mention of counseling. I hoped he would keep an open mind about it, but I wasn't going to push this early in the process.

Nancy didn't seem to notice his reaction, or maybe she saw it so often from patients that it barely registered anymore. Instead, she asked, "Have you spoken with our financial department? Your insurance will likely cover the testing, but the actual procedures and medications aren't usually covered. We have access to loans, medical credit cards and even grants if that's something you'll want to investigate with one of our financial counselors."

Fully aware that we were incredibly lucky when it came to money, I had a moment of guilt as I said, "That's not an issue for us. We'll be self-paying for whatever our insurance doesn't cover."

"Well, that makes things simpler," Nancy replied, shutting the folder filled with forms and pamphlets. Handing it over, she said, "Dr. Tafesh will be in to see you in a few minutes. She's finishing up with another patient."

Alone in the office, Ivan spoke first. "I'll go if you want to go." He cleared his throat. "To therapy."

I shifted in my seat and touched his jaw. He seemed so uncomfortable in this space, surrounded by plastic models and tasteful infographics of male and female reproductive systems. "I appreciate that, Ivan."

He grunted in that adorable grumpy bear way he had. "It's the least I can do."

"It's really not," I countered and stroked his jaw, feeling the slight scratch of stubble under my fingertips. "I know this isn't how we wanted this to go, and I wish my uterus would behave and do its job because—"

"Stop." He silenced me with a tender kiss. Pressing his forehead to mine, he said, "Whatever happens, whatever is wrong, we'll figure it out together, yes?"

Basking in his love for me, I nodded and stole a quick kiss as the door opened behind us. We both stood to greet Dr. Tafesh, shaking her hand and introducing ourselves. She had the most incredible tawny eyes and a friendly smile that set me at ease. Her earrings caught my attention, and I couldn't help but tap my own similar golden earrings. "Zoya?"

"Yes!" Dr. Tafesh answered excitedly. "I see you're a fan as well."

"Yes. Very much so." I couldn't wait to tell Zoya I had seen her designs out in the wild.

"Why don't we have a seat and chat about your medical history?"

After we sat, Ivan kept one arm around my shoulders, and the other reached for my hand, holding it as we waited for Dr. Tafesh to scroll through her tablet screen. "You're both in very good health. Erin, you're in your prime reproductive years, and Ivan," she pronounced his name the correct way with a long "e" sound, "you're a bit older but still within the optimal range for conception."

Ivan's jaw twitched at the "bit older" remark. He was nearly ten years my senior, after all.

"Ivan, you seem to exercise quite a lot," Dr. Tafesh remarked as she read our intake forms. "A minimum of twenty-four hours a week! Are you a professional athlete?"

"I operate a mixed martial arts gym," he explained, "so I

stay in fighting shape."

"I see." She glanced back down at the tablet. "Erin, you take a more moderate approach it seems."

"Just barre and some light lifting and cardio at home," I confirmed.

"Your cycles are regular," she commented. "Low pain levels with your period. No heavy cramping or bleeding?"

"No."

"You have a family history of endometriosis," she murmured. "Mother and grandmother?"

"Yes."

"And you've never been pregnant and miscarried?"

"No."

"Well, you two are a puzzle," Dr. Tafesh announced with a smile. "I like a good puzzle." Sitting back in her chair, she placed the tablet on her lap. "So, I would like to start with a wide range of blood tests for both of you and then some imaging studies for Erin. Ivan, we'll need a sample from you. The results from these tests will help me form a better idea of what the problem might be and how best to go about fixing it. Do you two have any questions for me?"

I did, of course, and opened up the list of them in the Notes app on my phone. I asked them one by one, and Dr. Tafesh answered every one of them in a way that was easy to understand and set my mind at ease. After our consultation, we were walked to an imaging room across the hall for my ultrasounds and then to the lab for our bloodwork. I had to stifle a laugh at the unamused look on Ivan's face when the lab tech handed him a paper bag with a sample cup inside.

"Down the hall, to the right," the tech said, gesturing that direction. "Pick a room. Read the instructions in the bag or on the posters on the wall. After you give your sample, tighten the lid, write the time on the label, put the cup in the bag, and drop it off at the sample window. Once that's done, you're free to go."

"Is he serious?" Ivan hissed when we were out in the hallway. He stared at the bag in his hand as if it were filled with something offensive. "They want me to…" He couldn't even finish the thought. "Here?"

Taking his hand, I smiled coyly and tugged him forward. "Come on."

"Erin," he protested but followed along anyway.

"It's going to be fine," I assured him. "You'll see."

He grumbled something in Russian I couldn't make out and trudged behind me until we reached one of the rooms reserved for giving a sample. I pulled him inside and locked the door behind us. Leaning back against it, I grinned. While I had been prepping for our first visit, I had joined an infertility group on Facebook. It was filled with lots of great information and tips for moments like this. Worried that Ivan would be uncomfortable in a setting like this, I had ordered something very special and new for the occasion. I was pretty sure he was going to like it.

He had stopped in the center of the room. His entire stance was tight, as if he were ready to bolt from the room and never come back. He grimaced when he noticed the TV mounted on the wall in front of a low couch covered in a shiny, easily cleaned navy blue vinyl. "I am not watching porn and stroking one out on a couch that squeaks."

"I can't do anything about the squeaky couch," I said, still leaning against the door, "but I can help with the other part."

Ivan's eyes narrowed with suspicion. "How?"

Wordlessly, I reached down and grasped the hem of my black pencil skirt. I had worn a typical work outfit today—pencil skirt, silk coral wrap blouse, and heels—but underneath I had a hidden secret. Holding his piqued interest, I pulled the hem of my skirt higher and higher, not stopping until it was bunched around my waist. Ivan's heated gaze burned right through me as he swallowed hard at the sight of my black thigh highs and the matching garter belt. The tiny panties were barely-there mesh.

When I untied the silk ties at my waist and opened my shirt to reveal a balconette bra, he tossed the paper bag onto the couch and stalked toward me. I giggled excitedly against his lips as he captured my mouth and then moaned when he lifted me into his arms and cupped my bottom. He laughed quietly and then gestured toward the sign on the back of the door. "We're supposed to be quiet."

"Right," I whispered, grabbing hold of his neck and the back of his head to kiss him aggressively. He growled deep in his chest, and I could already feel the rigid length of his cock growing between us. Gently and quietly as possible, he placed me on the couch and knelt between my open thighs. I rested my calves on his shoulders and lifted my backside to free the paper bag and sample cup trapped beneath me. He took the cup out and placed it on the top of the couch, leaning it against the wall where it would be easily grabbed when the time was right.

"We can't swap any body fluids down south," I reminded him and pointed to the poster on the wall above us.

"Not a fucking problem," he assured me as he freed his dick from his pants. He stroked his thick, long shaft with his scarred and tattooed hand. His monster cock looked normal in his big hands, but when I reached for him, wrapping my slim fingers around his girth, it looked obscenely huge. I rubbed my thumb along the underside of the ruddy head, pushing back his foreskin, and he groaned, thrusting his cock against my hand for more stimulation.

"Wait," I instructed breathlessly. "There's something else for you."

His eyes flashed with need. "Show me."

Widening my thighs even more, I ran my fingers along the thin triangle of fabric covering my pussy. Pushing the fabric apart, I whispered, "Look."

"Where the fuck did you get these?" He took advantage of the split fabric to trace my labia and then dip his fingers into me.

"That's my secret," I replied, starting to pant as his fingers swirled over my clit.

"You're buying more of these," he decided. "And you're wearing them to work so I can bend you over the desk in our office and fuck you whenever I want."

My pussy clenched at the image of him storming into the office, closing the door and pushing me face down on my desk. The idea of having my skirt shoved up, and his cock thrusting into while I gripped my desk made me so wet. He groaned again and pressed two of his big fingers inside of me, pumping in and out as I stroked his cock. He leaned over me and plundered my mouth, tangling his tongue with mine until we were both shaking and panting.

"I'm close," he gritted out. "Really fucking close."

I kept one hand on his cock and reached for the cup with the other. Careful not to put my fingers inside, I removed the lid and set it aside. It was a little tricky to hold the cup in place while I moved my hand faster and tighter over his shaft and right under the head where he was the most sensitive. "Come on, baby," I urged, my tongue tracing my upper lip. "Give me your cum."

"Fuck," he growled and thrust forward into my hand.

"That's it," I murmured breathily. "Fuck my hand. Show me how much you want to put a baby in me."

His pace stuttered. Harshly, he whispered, "Fuck. Fuck!"

"That's it. Give me every last drop," I urged, milking him with controlled strokes until his entire sample was in the cup. He was still shuddering when I grabbed the lid and carefully sealed the cup. I had barely set aside the cup when he jerked down both of my bra cups, baring my hard nipples to his hungry gaze. He licked both of them as he pushed three fingers into my pussy and circled my clit with his thumb. When he pinched my nipple, I arched my hips at the wild jolt of pain and pleasure. The moment he pinched my other nipple, I saw stars. Somehow, I managed to hold back a cry of pleasure, staying completely silent as an incredible orgasm overwhelmed me.

He slumped forward on top of me, his forehead between my breasts. I wrapped my arms around him and held him close, enjoying the heat and weight of him. After a while, when we had both stopped panting, he kissed me tenderly and stroked my face. "Thank you."

"No, no, no," I replied, still glowing after my climax.

"Thank *you.*"

He laughed and kissed me again. "Let's get out of here."

Glad for the attached bathroom, we quickly tidied up and labeled the cup. He placed it back in the paper bag before we left the sample room and dropped it off at the discreetly labeled little window. Hand in hand, we exited the clinic through the waiting room and took the elevator down to the parking garage.

"So," I said as he turned onto Fannin from the garage, "what's your idea about Ruby's job?"

His mouth quirked with a boyish grin. "She's going to work for me."

I blinked. "You can't be serious."

"I am."

"Ivan."

"Erin."

My mouth settled into an annoyed line. "You and Ruby working together will be a shit show."

"Probably," he agreed, "at first, but I think it will be good for her."

"That depends on what you expect her to do."

"Cleaning equipment, organizing weights, gym laundry, scheduling, inventory and anything else she can do to take some of the weight off your shoulders and mine," he said. "She can come with me in the mornings to open up while I work out."

I snorted. "You leave the house before five."

"Yes. And?"

"She's like a hibernating bear when she's asleep. Good luck getting her out of bed on time."

"She'll get up and go to work, or she'll have to deal with her probation officer," he replied matter-of-factly. "She's an adult. She can set her own alarm and take responsibility for herself." He glanced over at me before switching lanes. "She doesn't have very many options. She can take a temp job through one of the programs that hire ex-cons, or she can come work with us in the family business. Maybe it's not the career she wants, but it's steady work. The pay will be fair. She'll have insurance—"

"And she'll be safe," I interrupted, finally understanding why he wanted her at the gym with us. "We'll both be safe with you all day. You won't have to worry as much because we'll be in your line of sight."

"Exactly," he replied. "I need you both close until we get this situation handled."

"We as in you and me and Ruby? Or we meaning you and Nikolai and the others?"

"Yes," he answered, shooting me a playful smile.

"Ivan!" I huffed.

"Erin," he said more seriously, "this is a very delicate situation, right? We're talking about a criminal conspiracy inside the jail—rape and who knows what else because Ruby won't tell us the rest. We don't know how high this thing goes. If Ruby isn't willing to go to the authorities and press charges—and I don't blame her—we are limited in what we can do and how we can cover ourselves."

"I know," I agreed tiredly. "It's such a mess." I bit my lower lip. "What she told us about—the little she told us—is sex trafficking. It's illegal as fuck. Maybe," I hesitated, "maybe we should call the Texas Rangers or the FBI."

Ivan looked at me as if I had suddenly sprouted three heads. "Please, tell me you're joking."

"I'm not. The Texas Rangers investigate this sort of thing. That's part of their mandate, isn't it? To investigate corruption?"

"What makes you think they aren't corrupt, too?"

I shrugged. "They're the Texas Rangers. They're the good guys."

"As much as I would like to believe in romantic notions like that, I think it's best if we don't do something that drastic yet." With a shake of his head, he added, "It's not our decision. Ruby has to decide who she wants to tell and when. We can't force that on her."

"No, you're right." Ruby had been clear she didn't want to go public about her experience. "You're right."

"Erin, look at me."

I did.

"I don't care what it costs or how many lines I have to cross. I will get justice for your sister. It might not be the legal kind, but she's going to get it," he promised.

I could only hope that the lines he might have to cross wouldn't send him to prison.

CHAPTER THIRTEEN

IVAN STOOD AT the counter the next morning, dumping scoops of protein powder into the blender, when Ruby unhappily shuffled into the kitchen. He plopped the lid onto the blender and pressed the button. "Good morning!"

Frowning, Ruby grunted and yanked open the refrigerator. She grabbed a bottle of orange juice and then scowled at the blender until he turned it off. She grimaced when he started to pour it into his tumbler. "What the hell is that?"

"It's my protein shake."

She plunked down the container of orange juice and picked up the giant canister of protein powder. As she read the ingredients, she made a face. "How can you drink this crap? Vegan? And what the hell is a BCAA?"

"I drink it because it's a quick and consistent way to get enough protein in my diet. I use vegan because the ingredients are higher quality, and they do more safety testing." He took the canister from her and put it back in its cabinet. "Block chain amino acids."

"What?"

"BCAA," he clarified. "They're amino acids our bodies can't produce. We can only get them from food or supplements."

She seemed surprised as she admitted, "I had no idea you were, you know, educated in nutrition."

"I can even count to twenty without taking off my shoes and socks." With a shake of his head, he started drinking his protein shake.

"Yeah? But what about twenty-one? Do you have to take off your pants to go that high?"

Ivan choked on a mouthful of the thick liquid at her unexpected joke. She laughed at his predicament and snatched a dishtowel from next to the sink. She smacked him with it. "Here."

"Thanks." He mopped his face and then whacked her right back with it. "I could have choked to death."

She rolled her eyes. "I totally would have pushed you over onto your side and called 9-1-1 as soon as I finished my juice."

"Wow. Such compassion and caring," he grunted.

"You're the one who made me get up at this ungodly hour. You get uncaring Ruby this time of the morning."

"You're more than welcome to go right back to bed and spend the rest of your day trying to get a job washing restaurant dishes or scrubbing hotel toilets."

"Pass." She opened a cabinet and grabbed a glass before sloshing orange juice into it. "When do you eat real food?"

"Erin brings breakfast, or I make it at the gym in the kitchenette at the back." He gestured to the pantry. "You can bring things you like and keep them there. Tell Erin what you like, and she'll make sure it's stocked at the gym. For lunch, we go out or have something delivered. I leave that up to Erin."

"You really like letting her boss you around, huh?" Ruby's eyebrows rose as she drank her juice in unladylike gulps. Her eyes narrowed. "Is that your thing?"

"My thing?"

"Yeah." She gestured with her hand. "Your kink. Having some pretty little thing give you orders and, well, you know."

He huffed out an annoyed breath. "We aren't talking about this."

"I knew it!" she declared triumphantly.

"You don't know shit," he replied, swiping the orange juice jug and returning it to the refrigerator.

"Uh-huh." She grinned as if she had figured out a difficult riddle. "We'll see."

"Go ahead and ask Erin." He grabbed his tumbler and polished off the last of his shake. "Be sure you really want to know," he warned. "You won't be able to forget the mental pictures she paints."

"Gross." Ruby acted as if she were gagging. She placed her empty glass on the top rack of the dishwasher and took his tumbler from him, placing it there also. "It's bad enough that I can hear you two if I don't get my headphones on fast enough." She puffed up her chest and dramatically imitated his voice. "Oh, Erin. Oh, *angel moy.*"

"Oh, fuck off," he swore, laughing despite himself. "I do not sound like that."

"Bro," she said seriously. "Would I lie?"

He snorted. "Do you want me to answer that?"

She shot him the finger. "Are we going to work or what?"

"Let's go."

The ride to work was surprisingly pleasant. It was the longest time he had ever been alone with Ruby without the buffer of Erin between them. He had to wonder if confessing to Erin about what had happened to her in jail had somehow freed the real Ruby. She seemed much more like the younger woman Erin had described to him.

"Did you schedule your classes yet?"

"The drug offender ones?"

"Yes."

"Not yet," she admitted, scratching at her knee through her black leggings. "There's a class toward the end of February. I think I'll try to get into that one."

"How long is it?"

"Five days. Three hours each day."

He frowned. "That's a bullshit schedule."

"Right?" She shook her head. "Like people who just got out of jail can afford to take five days off from work or to ask to be rescheduled if they just got a new job!"

"The people who make these laws have never had to deal with that kind of situation. They make their decisions in a vacuum."

"Clearly," she agreed. "So, boss, I'm going to need five days off in February and a ride to and from class."

"Take it up with my supervisor," he counseled.

"Is that how it is? Like—not joking right now."

"I hate the business part of the gym," he admitted. "Erin has a natural skill for all of that. Bringing her into the business was the second smartest decision I ever made."

"And the first?"

"Marrying her." He expected her tease or poke fun at him, but she didn't. She seemed to be pleased with his answer.

"I always thought she would end up following in Dad's footsteps. I think that's why she liked Teague. He reminded her of Dad. At first," she added.

"But later?"

"Later, she figured out what a colossal dick he was. Not that she'll ever admit that," Ruby insisted. "She hates to speak badly of people. She always wants to believe the best of them. She went out of her way to end things on friendly terms with him." Reaching into her purse, she said, "I'm glad she found you. She deserves to be with someone who loves her the way you do."

He wasn't sure how to respond to her unexpected compliment. Finally, he said, "I would do anything for her."

"I know you would." She unwrapped a stick of gum and popped it in her mouth. Turning her attention out the window, she stared into the early morning darkness. "Andrei loved me the same way," she said, her voice so soft he barely heard the words. She glanced back at him and advised, "Remember how our story ended."

For the rest of the drive, he could think of nothing else. She didn't mean the drug addiction part of their story. She meant the part where Andrei died and left her behind. He couldn't allow his story with Erin to end that way. He refused.

When they reached the Warehouse, he walked her through his morning routine for opening up the gym. In a few days, he would expect her to take over that duty. He showed her the supply closet and the laminated checklists Erin had put together for cleaning the equipment, washing laundry and more.

"Towels get washed three or four times a day, depending on how quickly the hampers outside the locker rooms fill up." He showed her the correct settings for the washer and dryer as well as the types and amounts of laundry detergents, bleach, and everything else Erin had on the laundry checklist. "Brooms and mops are over there."

"Do I need to mop the whole place?" Ruby asked, eyes wide at the prospect of having all that square footage to clean.

"No, we only mop if someone gets sick or there's a spilled drink or something like that. We have a cleaning crew that comes in every night to clean and sanitize the floors, mats, equipment and locker rooms. Paco stays late for that." He led her to the private bathroom he had installed for Erin when she started working at the gym. "There is an extra key to this door in Erin's top drawer. Make sure to lock it when you're done. The guys here are fucking animals."

"Duly noted," she said, making a face.

"Kitchen and break room are here." He showed her to the large lounging space at the rear of the gym. "Fridge. Water. Coffee. Cups. Plates. Silverware. Pots. Pans." He opened and closed cabinets and drawers to show her where to find things. He tapped a laminated sign on the fridge about labeling food. "Erin cleans out the refrigerator every week. She keeps labels and markers here." He pointed to the metal basket fixed to the side of the appliance. "If it's not labeled with a name and the date it went into the refrigerator, it gets thrown away."

"Good. God." Ruby shook her head. "I thought she was bossy when we were kids, but this is bananas."

"In her defense, this place was a pigsty before she came in and laid down the law." He rubbed the back of his neck, grimacing at the memory of her gagging the first time she opened the refrigerator in here. "Her rules and organization can be a bit much sometimes, but her system works. Look at this place. It's spotless."

"Fair enough," Ruby said.

He continued the tour by taking her to each piece of equipment, all of the weight stations, the mats, the sparring rings and the cages. "Everyone who trains here is supposed to clean up after themselves. Most of them do, but they get fatigued and forget. If you see a station that's been used and not cleaned, spray and wipe." He pointed out the bottles of cleaner and the stacks of paper towels placed near every station. "The biggest issue for the gym is preventing staph. That shit is dangerous There are fighters who have died because of staph infections that started in a cut or scrap and spread. Cleanliness is the first and best defense."

"Right," she said, nodding and taking it seriously. "There was a staph outbreak in one of the cell blocks when I first went inside. One of the girls over there ended up with it on her face." She shuddered. "She almost lost her eye."

He wasn't at all surprised to hear that. He had seen even worse things in prison, but he wasn't about to share those stories with her. Instead, he asked, "Any questions?"

"*Nyet*, comrade," she said with a mocking salute.

"Oh, for fuck's sake," he grumbled and walked away from her. "I'm already regretting hiring you."

"Hey, can I get an advance on my first check?" she called out as he unlocked the office he shared with Erin. "And what's the retirement plan here?"

Throughout the rest of the morning, he kept an eye on her. Erin wasn't coming in until after lunch because she had meetings at the bank, with their accountant and Mueller. That meant Ruby was the only woman in the Warehouse, and he worried that there might be friction. The few times he caught some of his fighters trying to catch Ruby's attention, he made sure they didn't look at her a second time.

"Why don't you just issue them blindfolds?" Ruby asked when she wandered into the kitchen a little while later. "The amount of sweat dripping on the floor from the laps you're making them run is making more work for me."

"More work means you have job stability," he replied, grabbing a dozen eggs from the well-stocked refrigerator. "Do you want one?"

She shook her head. "I made some oatmeal while you were stretching your neck in that torture machine."

"It's for neck strengthening."

"Whatever you say." She flopped down in a chair and watched him crack eggs into a bowl for his usual scramble. "Do you know how many times I've heard the words 'bitch tits' this morning?"

He frowned. "I'll talk to them about the language."

"You should have Erin make a sign," she joked. "Can you imagine? She'd need, like, twenty sheets of poster board to list all the forbidden words."

"In English," he remarked, still cracking eggs. "She would need even more for all the Spanish and Russian that gets thrown around in here."

"How many eggs is that?" Ruby asked in a scandalized tone. "Is this when you break out into song and tell me how you eat five dozen eggs so you can stay the size of a barge?"

His brow furrowed, and he turned to face her. "What the hell does that mean?"

She seemed taken aback. "Gaston? Belle? LeFou?"

He shook his head.

"Seriously?" She reacted with disbelief. "I'm supposed to believe that my sister married you, but she's never made you sit through *Beauty and the Beast* so many times the lyrics and music are imprinted in your brain for all eternity?"

"Is it a movie?"

"It's her *favorite* movie. The Disney cartoon version," she clarified. "She watched it every single day after school from kindergarten until, like, fifth grade. She watched it at least once a week after that. Burned through dozens of copies of the tape and the DVD." Her expression turned wistful. "We went to Disney World when we were kids, and I thought she was going to faint when she saw Belle. We were supposed to go back after they added all the restaurants and show to Magic Kingdom, but Mom and Dad…" She let the thought fade. "Well. Anyway." She stood up and checked her watch. "I need to switch out the laundry."

After she left, he finished cooking his breakfast and then used his phone to look up the movie. He added it to his watchlist and then texted Erin to see how her morning meetings were going. She had taken Kir with her, but he was still anxious that something would happen. She replied back with a selfie from the bank waiting area and assured him all was well.

Back out on the gym floor, he noticed the way Ruby carried herself as she moved around the space. She kept her back to the wall. Her eyes were continually scanning the room, seeking out potential threats and exits. He understood that fearful behavior and defensiveness. He had been the same way once. It was hard to slide back into civilian life after all that time on high alert.

He waited until she neared the mats where two of his fighters grappled and signaled for her to join him. She stopped at his side and watched them. He glanced down at her and asked, "Do you want to learn?"

Seemingly stunned by his question, she stared up at him with confusion. "What?"

"Do you want to learn to fight?"

She looked around as if she thought she were being set up for a prank. "But...you don't train women."

"You're family. It's different." He kept his arms crossed, and his jaw set. "It would be good for Erin to have a partner closer to her size."

"Why?"

"Why does Erin need a smaller partner than me?"

Ruby rolled her eyes. "Why are you offering to teach me?"

"Because you need to know how to defend yourself."

"From?"

"Anyone stupid enough to try you," he replied, glancing down at her with a wry smile.

She returned his grin. "Okay. I'm game."

He nodded. "Good. We'll start in the morning."

CHAPTER FOURTEEN

"**Y**OU SURE YOU want to go in there alone?" Kir asked as we rode the elevator to the top floor of James Mueller's headquarters.

"Yes."

Kir looked uneasy. "I promised Ivan I wouldn't let you out of my sight."

"I'm sure he didn't mean that literally."

"I'd rather not find out if I'm wrong."

"I'll be fine," I assured him. The hulking fighter and enforcer for Nikolai grunted unhappily at my decision, but he didn't argue further as we stepped out of the elevator and into the reception area of the firm. After I spoke with the receptionist, he directed us to a private waiting area outside of Mueller's office.

Just as we sat down on the sleek sable leather chairs, an indignant shout penetrated the office door in front of us. Kir and I exchanged surprised glances as the angry shouts continued. I wasn't able to decipher any of the actual words. The room was too well constructed, and the door was thick and heavy. Whatever was being said, it wasn't good.

The door burst open suddenly, and I was stunned to see Teague storming out of the office. He must have been just as shocked to see me because he froze right there in front of the open door. I took in the sight of his wrinkled suit and stained shirt. His hair was a mess, and his eyes were bloodshot with deep circles. He seemed on the verge of his losing his mind.

When Teague stepped toward me, Kir instantly rose from his seat and moved between us. With a click of his teeth, Kir gestured to the elevator. "Keep walking."

Teague didn't have the energy to argue. He dropped his gaze like a beat dog and left without a word. I stared after him, wondering what the hell he had gotten himself into and what it had to do with Mueller. The idea that Mueller might be connected to the attack on Zoya and me began to grow. Was that how Teague knew what was said to me during the attack? Had Mueller ordered it? Or was there some other shadowy hand at work?

I didn't have time to think of all consider all of those possibilities. The doors to the elevator had just closed when Mueller walked out of his office to greet me. His gaze jumped to Kir and then back to me. He extended his hand toward me and apologized. "I'm sorry about that. Teague is having a rough couple of weeks."

"Clearly," I replied dryly. "This is Kir. He's a good friend."

"Kir." Mueller extended his hand and flashed the briefest wince as Kir clamped his hand in a vise-like grip. He stepped aside and gestured for me to enter his office. "Whenever you're ready."

I didn't miss the way he tried to hide the flex of his fingers at his side. Hopefully, Kir hadn't actually broken any of them. Giving Kir a look, I indicated the seat he had just vacated, and he reluctantly sat. I walked into the office and was instantly drawn to the floor to ceiling windows overlooking Discovery Green. "This is quite a view, Mr. Mueller."

"James," he insisted. "And, yes, it is." He stopped next to me to enjoy the view. "I walked into this room, looked out these windows and decided I didn't need to waste time looking at any other buildings. This was the perfect one for my Houston expansion."

"You chose well."

"A smart man takes what he wants when he sees it."

A shiver of unease coursed down my spine. I studiously ignored his sidelong glance, not wanting to confirm my suspicion about his meaning. If he had any crazy ideas about me, he could fuck right off.

Taking a step away, I wandered over to a detailed model of the development he was proposing. It was very ambitious, combining recreation and entertainment with luxury and affordable housing and green spaces. A framed set of in-fographics showed the financials of the project as well as the benchmarks for each step of the development.

"You've known Teague a long time?" Mueller joined me at the model and wiped away a bit of dust with his thumb.

"Six years," I answered, continuing my trek around the edge of the model to maintain space between us. "We met in college."

"And dated, I understand."

"Yes. Briefly," I lied, not wanting to get into any kind of discussion about my dating history with a man I barely knew. "And you? How long have you known him?"

"His whole life."

Taken aback, I couldn't even hide my surprise. "Really?"

"His father and I served together."

The connection finally clicked. "Army Ranger, right?"

"Yes." He gestured to some photos behind his desk. "Two tours in Iraq and one in Afghanistan."

"Were you with his dad when the IED…?"

Mueller nodded solemnly. He tugged down the collar of his shirt to reveal a gnarly scar that I suspected traveled far down his chest. "I was close enough to get the shrapnel but far enough back that I survived."

"I'm sorry. That must have been a terrible day."

"It was." A phone chirped, and he slipped his hand into his pocket to retrieve it. He glanced at the screen. "I need to take this."

"I can step out," I offered.

"No, you stay." He swiped the screen and lifted the phone to his ear while walking toward a door on the other side of his office. "Hang on…"

The door closed behind him, and I indulged my curiosity about the photos behind his desk. There were the usual photos of his family including his very cute kids. From the looks of it, they were a family who liked the outdoors. There were photos from camping trips and hikes and early morning snapshots of two of his young sons in camouflage hunting gear in what looked to be a deer blind.

Seeing Teague standing with Mueller and his family in so many of the photos left me questioning everything I knew about him. He had never—not once—said anything racist in my presence. He had more friends who were black or Middle Eastern or Asian than he did who were white. His sister had converted to Judaism to marry her longtime boyfriend. He had been nothing but supportive of Abby and was a loving uncle to Abby and Jacob's little girls.

Was it possible he truly believed the shit that Mueller did? Was it possible for someone to hide those feelings that well? Had I dated a man with so much hate in his heart?

Troubled by the idea that I never even knew Teague, I moved along to the other photos. There was a selection from his years in the military, some stateside and others overseas. Some of the same faces from his time in the Army reappeared in more recent photos at the same camping lodge where he took his family. As I looked closer, I noticed the almost hidden details in the carved railing lining the front porch of the rustic cabin.

Are you kidding me?

There was no mistaking what I was seeing. Lightning bolts, runes, eagles and other hate symbols were used in such a way that they seemed innocuous. Almost pretty, I admitted reluctantly. If I hadn't researched the world Mueller belonged to in preparation for this meeting, I wouldn't have known there were other meanings to these symbols.

Another photo showed the name of the private riverside camp. My stomach churned when I read the sign. Wannsee River Camp. What kind of monster named their camp after the infamous Wannsee Conference?

"Sorry about that," Mueller apologized as he returned to the office. "What do you think about the camp?"

"It's very beautiful," I said, thinking it was a shame such a pristine natural landscape had been soiled by his ugly ideas. "Hill Country?" I guessed.

"Bandera County," he confirmed. "You and Ivan should

come out and stay with us some weekend." He delivered his invitation as he came to stand beside me.

I suppressed a shudder at his closeness. "We aren't very outdoorsy people."

"You might change your mind in the right company." He glanced over at me, his smile unnervingly charming. "I think you two would fit right in with our kind of people."

"And what kind is that?" I dared to ask, wondering if he was about to come right out with his white pride speech.

"People with shared values," he said, skirting the real issue. "We love God, our country, our families, and our communities. We work hard. We contribute to society. We're the very best this nation has to offer." Clearly trying to test me, he asked, "You believe in those things, don't you?"

"Yes, of course. Although we aren't religious."

"Maybe you haven't found the right church yet."

"No, that's not the problem." Before he could try to rope me into a theological discussion, I left the wall of photos and returned to the development model. Hoping to turn his attention to the project in front of us, I traced a blank area in his development plan between two larger buildings. It confirmed what I had suspected. He needed our property to ensure his development had uninterrupted flow. "This is our property right here. One of them," I amended. "One we might be willing to sell."

"If?" he probed.

"If the price is right, of course. And I do mean right," I added with a pointed look. "It's clear this an important piece of land in your proposed development. We won't be letting it go for anything less than market."

"I might be able to offer you something else in exchange for a lower sale price," he suggested. "Maybe a piece of the equity partnership?"

"That might be something that interests Ivan," I replied. Even though it was a tempting offer and one that would increase our net worth substantially, Ivan had been very clear that he had absolutely no intention of doing any sort of business with Mueller. I was to come here, make nice, and then regretfully decline the offer to do business.

Mueller smiled as if he had already won. "I'm sure we can work something out to your satisfaction."

I plucked a business card from my purse and handed it to him. "Send me some numbers, and we'll talk."

"I look forward to negotiating with you."

"We'll see." I took one of the glossy brochures from the end of the table and tucked it into my purse on the way out the door. Kir stood as soon as he saw me, and we headed straight for the elevator, neither of us looking back.

As the elevator descended, I couldn't shake the weird feeling of being alone with a man who seemed so boringly normal but who held such hateful, evil ideas. How many other people did I cross paths with every single day who believed the same vile things?

"So," Kir said after we were safely inside my SUV, "was it like the Berghof in there?"

I shot him a strange look. "You sure know a lot about Nazis."

"History Channel," he explained. "I have trouble sleeping, and that's usually the only interesting shit on television. It's all World War II, ancient aliens and conspiracy theories."

"Well, sorry to let you down, but his office was exactly what you would expect from any CEO. Black leather. Lots of metal. Blond wood tones. Bland as hell."

"Huh," Kir remarked, seemingly stumped. "I guess I thought he would be more…" He trailed off as he searched for the right word. "Villainous."

I huffed with amusement. "You mean, like, Dr. Evil? A lair or something?"

"I don't know. Maybe."

"Okay, Kir, I hope that if Ivan asks you to work as my babysitter again you accept because the conversations we've had today have been an absolute treat." All day he had surprised me with witty observations and funny stories. "Tell me about these ancient aliens…"

Kir enthusiastically launched into a lecture about the Book of Genesis, the Book of Ezekiel and Urim and Thummim. He had circumstantial evidence to back up his wild theories, things like the Nazca Lines and pictograms in the Urals. By the time we arrived at the Warehouse, I was honestly starting to doubt the accepted history of the pyramids.

"I'll send you some links," he promised. "Get ready to fall down the alien rabbit hole," he called out before getting into his truck and heading home.

Amused by his slightly unhinged theories but also the tiniest bit anxious that aliens really did walk among us, I entered the Warehouse and removed my sunglasses. The afternoon training blocks were well underway, and the sounds of men grappling, coaches barking orders, and the aggressive music Ivan preferred after lunch echoed off the high ceilings.

Ivan was easy to find. His deep voice carried over the others as he clapped his hands and called a stop to the grappling happening on the mats. Barefooted, he stepped onto the mats and tapped the shoulder of the newest fighter to join our camp. Davor had come to Houston with his older brother Dragan who had signed to play with the Rockets. Both brothers were big. Dragan, the basketball player, was taller than Ivan, Sergei, and Ten. He sometimes came to the Warehouse to work out or watch Davor train.

Cody, the fighter who had been training with Davor, took a water break. Ivan slipped into his place and began to teach and correct Davor. In moments like this, watching the way he patiently explained and practiced with his fighters, I saw a glimpse of our future as parents. Ivan was so ready to be a father, and I hoped with every fiber of my being that someday I would stand here on the edge of the gym floor and watch him teach our son or daughter how to defend themselves.

I spotted Ruby coming out of the utility room with a stack of freshly laundered towels. She placed them on the shelves outside the locker rooms and took the hamper crammed with dirty towels back to the washers. Pleasantly surprised to see her working so hard, I made my way across the gym to the office.

My feet were aching, and I dropped into my desk chair and kicked off my red suede pumps. They were a gorgeous pair of shoes, but they murdered my arches and pinky toes. I flexed my feet and sighed with relief, all the while wondering if I could convince Ivan to rub my feet later. Of course, he would start with my feet and end up with his hands somewhere much higher.

"Hey! You're back." Ruby swept into the office. She picked

up my purse from the chair where I had left it and sat down with it on her lap. "How were all your meetings?"

"Boring, but at least, I had Kir with me for entertainment."

"He's funny?"

"He is."

"He talks?" She narrowed her eyes. "Like actual words?"

"Yes."

"Are you sure? Because when I met him the other day, he grunted and that's it."

I shrugged. "Sounds like that's more on you than him."

"What could he possibly have to talk about that you would find interesting?"

"Ancient astronauts."

"Oh, come on!" Ruby laughed. "Really?"

"Yep. He's sending me some links later."

"Oh, lord! Please promise me you're not going to turn into one of those Area 51 loonies!"

"No promises. He had some convincing arguments."

She shook her head. "And so it begins."

Laughing, I signed into the gym's email and started sorting through my inbox. "What do you think of working here?"

"It's okay."

I could tell she was trying to play it cool so I didn't push. "Nobody has hassled you?"

She rolled her eyes. "Ivan laid down the law."

I grinned. "Yeah, he's like that."

"Overprotective?"

"Yes." I tried to concentrate on the emails in my inbox, but I couldn't stop thinking about Teague. Needing to tell someone, I said, "I saw Teague."

She frowned. "Where?"

"At Mueller's office."

"Teague was with that Himmler wannabe?"

"Yes! I mean—that's weird, right? Did you ever…? Like…did I just not see it?"

"I told you he was trouble. Do you remember? Your second date, right? I told you that he was hiding something, and you wouldn't listen."

"To be fair, your judgment wasn't exactly the best at the time."

"Neither was yours considering how Teague turned out," she shot back.

Instead of being mad, I smiled. "It's kind of nice to sit here and have you snark back at me."

She rolled her eyes. "You are so sappy."

"And?"

"Don't expect me to start talking about my feelings."

"Wouldn't dream of it."

She stood up, put my purse back on the seat, and wandered over to the security system monitors. "Do you think he's in on it?"

"Who? Teague?"

She nodded. "You told me knew what those men said to you in the parking lot attack. He wasn't there, obviously, because you would have recognized him, but he may know the guys who did it. Maybe they're Mueller's guys, too."

"Maybe," I said, thinking she was probably right. "Do you think the guard who hurt you—Kavanaugh—is part of Mueller's organization?"

She turned away, putting all of her attention on the monitors. After a tense moment, she said, "He has a pair of lightning bolts on his chest and 1488 on his neck, under his collar. There was something else on his leg, but I never got a clear look at it."

She never got a clear look at it while she was being raped.

My heart broke, and my stomach ached painfully at the way my sister had suffered. I rose from my seat and crossed the office to stand by her. She roughly wiped the tears from her eyes but let me embrace her. I didn't know what to say. There weren't any words that could take away her pain and trauma. I could only hope that showing her love would ease some of her sufferings.

"There were others," she whispered, clinging to me so tightly I knew there would be bruises where her fingers had been. "Other women and other guards."

I hadn't told her about the voicemail yet. "On New Year's Eve, while we were at Denim and Diamonds, I got a voicemail from a number I didn't recognize. I didn't hear it until the next morning, but it was a woman. She was crying and begging for help and mercy. She was being beaten, I think, and probably worse."

Her arms tightened even more, squeezing me so hard I could hardly draw breath into my lungs. Trembling, she confessed, "They filmed it."

My heartbeat stuttered. "Filmed the rapes?"

"Yes," she answered, crying harder. "To sell. On the black market."

I couldn't even imagine what type of depraved mind wanted to watch rapes and beatings.

"But only of the women who were waiting for ICE."

"What do you mean?" I managed to free myself enough to stare into her face. "You mean, like, immigration?"

"Yeah." She wiped her face. "I heard about it when I was in the infirmary. There were two women in the beds next to mine, and they were talking about one of their friends going missing somewhere in the jail. They were speaking Spanish, so maybe they assumed I wouldn't understand, or maybe they were hoping I would so someone else would know."

"How do you go missing in jail? Aren't there roll calls? Cameras monitoring everything?"

"I think that's why they stick with the women who are waiting to be transferred to immigration for deportation," she explained. "It's easier to lose someone like that."

"And then those women get sent home, and no one will ever hear their stories."

"Exactly."

"Did they only target those women? Why did he go after you?"

She seemed to waver between telling the truth and refusing to speak. Closing her eyes, she confessed, "I did something so stupid."

"Hey," I said, rubbing her back, "it's okay, Ruby. Whatever it was, it doesn't matter. Okay? I only care about keeping you safe and putting a stop to what's happening inside the jail."

"You're going to be so fucking angry with me," she whined and starting crying harder. "You've been so supportive and proud of me and I fucked up so bad and I've been lying the whole time."

Over her shoulder, I noticed Ivan coming into the office. He took one step into the room, saw the situation and put up both hands. Silently, he backed away and closed the door with the barest hint of a click as the lock caught. Safe inside and our privacy guaranteed, I grabbed her hand and led her to the small couch on the far wall of the office. Tugging her down next to me, I held both hands and waited for her to look me in the eye. "Ruby, I will still love you and support you and be proud of you no matter what you tell me."

She sniffled and wiped at her eyes again. It took her a while to work up the courage, but I didn't mind. I held her hands and waited. Eventually, she lifted her head and admitted, "I was getting high inside."

Relief washed over me. "Is that all?"

"Is that all?" she echoed. "I'm telling you I used drugs inside after I was forced to get clean, and you don't think it's that big of a deal?"

"I'm sorry," I hastily replied, not wanting to piss her off and cause her to clam up again. "I was expecting something so much worse, but a relapse that early in your recovery isn't unexpected, especially in a high-stress environment."

She looked at me funny. "Ivan wasn't kidding. You have been reading a shit ton of books about addiction."

"I want to understand what you're going through and how to help you, Ruby. I love you, and I want you to be happy and fulfilled and not have this fucking demon following you around for the rest of your life."

"It's always going to be there, Erin. Addiction doesn't go away. It's a disease. It gets easier to not think about using and to not crave the high, but it's always there in the back of my mind."

"I'm sorry. You're right. I don't understand it the way you

do, but I'll try. If you share with me when you're struggling, I'll help any way I can. I promise, Ruby." I squeezed her hands. "I will not let you down ever again."

"What? Erin! You never let me down!"

"I did, Ruby." The guilt I had been carrying around for a long time came crashing down around me. "I was so wrapped up in my own life, in enjoying college and dating and going out with friends. I didn't want to deal with your problems." Hating myself for what I was about to admit, I started crying, too. "I blamed you for Mom and Dad. I was so angry with you. So, I told myself I didn't care and that you weren't my problem. I should have been a better sister."

"No, no, no," Ruby said, throwing her arms around me. "You've always been the best sister. I blamed myself for Mom and Dad. Of course, you did, too! We were so young, and we had no idea how to handle the trauma of losing them like that. I lost myself in pills and cocaine, and whatever else I could find to send me into the oblivion and numb my pain. You lost yourself in school and work and your friends."

"I tried to stay busy so I wouldn't have time to think about it," I realized, suddenly putting together all the pieces.

"And I'm glad that's the path you took," Ruby insisted. "I'm glad you stayed away from the shit that almost killed me." She rubbed her face with both hands. "The shit that got me into all this trouble I'm in now." Lowering her hands, she explained, "One of the girls on my cell block had a connection inside. I'm pretty sure it's one of the guards who brings in the drugs and cell phones and contraband. She offered me a free taste, and I resisted—at first. Then, one day, I got the shit knocked out of me by this big bully bitch, and I started thinking about how many more months I had to go, and I lost it. I wanted to forget everything."

"So, you accepted her offer?"

"Yes."

"And then?"

"It wasn't the pills I preferred. It was fentanyl. It was a huge fucking dose, way too much for the first time, at least." Ashamed, she shook her head. "We did the deal in a supply closet by the laundry, and I passed out almost as soon as I put the pill under my tongue. When I woke up, I was alone in the dark—and then he found me."

"Kavanaugh?"

"Yes."

"And he…?"

She nodded. "Twice." She closed her eyes and breathed out slowly. "After that, he would take me out of my cell whenever he wanted. A few weeks ago, before I got moved to the processing center to leave the jail, he had taken me to a room that I had never seen. It was in a part of the jail I had never been to or even knew existed."

When she stopped, I understood that she needed a moment to gather herself. I held onto her hand, and she started to speak again. "There was a camera on a tripod. Like the kind beauty influencers use to film their makeup tutorials," she explained. "What he did to me had been terrible before that, but the idea of him recording it so he could watch it or share it broke me. I didn't even try to fight him, and that just made him angrier." She winced. "I could barely walk the next morning."

"Oh, Ruby," I cried. "Oh my God."

She inhaled a shaky breath. "He kept me in the room for too long. We heard men's voices, and he dragged me into a storage room. He used duct tape to wrap up my wrists and ankles and covered my mouth with it so I couldn't make any noise or try to catch anyone's attention." She rubbed her mouth as if remembering the feeling of the tape. "The men had one of the girls with an ICE hold. She was younger than you. There were four or five men. Maybe more. I couldn't see them. I could only hear them."

I tried to visualize the picture she painted with her description. It must have been terrifying, like something out of a horror film. Part of me wanted to ask her to stop her story, to leave it unfinished so I wouldn't have the rest of the image in my head, but I didn't. I let her purge all the terrible things that had happened.

"They brutalized that girl. It was vile. She screamed and cried and begged. I couldn't do anything. I was useless."

"There was nothing you could have done," I desperately tried to assuage her guilt. "You were one woman against all those men."

"I know, but I can still hear her crying," she sobbed. "It was awful, Erin. So awful." She sniffled loudly. "And then…"

"Then?"

"She bit one of them. His dick," she clarified. "He shrieked, and then all hell broke loose. I didn't see it, but I heard it. I heard what they did to her." She aggressively rubbed her face. "I can still hear it." She blew out a shuddery breath. "And then it was quiet. Too quiet."

"They killed her?" I asked aghast. "They murdered her in jail?"

"Yes. They panicked. I could hear them fighting with each other and talking about the body. Kavanaugh was just as scared. He was terrified they were going to find us in the storage room. He had his hands over my mouth so hard that the insides of my lips were bleeding from the pressure of my teeth grinding into them." She traced her mouth as if reliving the memory. "When they were done, and it got quiet, he took me out of the room and returned me to my cell. He warned me not to say a word—or else."

I tried to process everything. "What happened to the girl they killed?"

"The next morning, during roll call, they found her hanging in her cell."

"They faked a suicide?"

"Yes."

"Holy shit." I sat back on the sofa and exhaled slowly. "Okay. So. Kavanaugh must have snitched, right? Because if he wanted to keep you quiet, he would have come after me on his own."

"But there was a whole team that came after you," she murmured, following my line of thought. "It was probably the other guards in their rape ring."

"One of them put his hand between my legs," I revealed. "He was disgusting. I can completely buy that he is a predator."

"So, what are we saying, Erin? That Teague is tied in with a rape ring that operates inside a jail? That he knows one of those guards?" She shuddered. "Or maybe he's one of their customers? Maybe he buys their sick films?"

"Oh, God," I said, feeling nauseated. "I hope not."

"This is really complicated, Erin." Ruby seemed over-whelmed by it all. "Teague. The guards. The dead girl. The Neo-Nazi angle."

"Somehow, it all fits together."

We sat shoulder to shoulder, both of us quietly contemplating what the hell we were supposed to do next. We would have to start by telling Ivan everything. He would be furious when he heard the whole story. Murderous, even. The possibility that Ivan would track down Kavanaugh and make him disappear didn't upset me as much as it probably should have. For what he had done to my sister, Kavanaugh deserved to be punished—and much harder than the justice system would allow.

"You want to come with me to a meeting?" Ruby unexpectedly asked.

Surprised by her question, I asked, "Really?"

"Yeah. Really." She seemed calmer as she explained, "I think it would be a good idea for me to get to a meeting today. I'm feeling stressed out and anxious, and I know where my thoughts are going to turn later when I'm alone."

Ready to do anything to help her maintain her sobriety, I stood up and reached for my purse. "Let's go."

"Now?"

"Yes. Now. I don't know where the meetings are, so you'll have to find one that starts soon." I grabbed her hand and tugged her off the couch. "Come on."

We had taken less than ten steps before Ivan intercepted us. Concerned, he asked, "Everything okay, *zolotse*?"

"Yep," I answered brightly.

He noticed the purse in my hand. "Where are you going?"

"To a meeting."

"A meeting?"

"Yes."

"Where?"

"We're not sure yet." I glanced back at Ruby, who had her phone in hand to find one. "But, it's probably at a church."

"A church." He looked between us as if we had lost our minds. "Are you sure you're okay?"

"Yes."

He glanced around the gym. "Let me have Paco or Ken take over. I'll drive you two."

"No." It felt surprisingly good to say it.

"No?" He frowned. "Why not?"

"Because I'm tired of letting these cowardly assholes control my life," I explained matter-of-factly. A surge of bravery had me lifting my chin. "I'm not going to run around afraid of my shadow anymore. I'm not going to limit myself or drag around a babysitter."

Ivan's mouth settled into a grim line. He seemed to be fighting the urge to argue with me. I couldn't blame him. He loved me as much as I loved him, and I wouldn't want him in danger either. Finally, he exhaled roughly. "Okay."

Surprised, I repeated, "Okay?"

He nodded. "*Da.* You're right. I can't coddle you. I can't clip your wings and put you in a cage." He stepped closer, sliding one hand from my waist to the small of my back and cupping my nape with the other. "Be careful. Stay alert. Try to be home before it gets dark. If you see anything that makes you nervous, you call 9-1-1 immediately."

"I will." I rose on tiptoes to kiss him. His warm hands held me in place a few more seconds before he reluctantly took his mouth from mine. "I'll see you at the house later."

"Text me with updates."

"I will." I backed away from him and waved. "*Ya lyublyu tebya.*"

Ivan smiled at my surprisingly good Russian. "I love you, baby."

Out in my SUV, I waited for Ruby to finish buckling her belt. As I shifted into reverse, I said, "We're going to embrace our inner Stabler and Benson. We're going to look into Mueller, Teague, Kavanaugh, and all of their asshole friends. We're going to dig up everything we can on them. We're going to build the biggest, nastiest, ugliest report—and then we're going to use it to fuck them."

Ruby's eyes widened, and then she grinned. "Hell. Yes."

CHAPTER FIFTEEN

I VAN WATCHED ERIN and Ruby leave the gym. He felt a sliver of guilt knowing that Kostya's spiders were following Erin and her sister. He was glad that Erin felt empowered, that she wasn't going to cower, but he wouldn't have let her leave without a guard if he hadn't known that Kostya had her under observation.

Seconds after Erin and Ruby left the gym, his phone vibrated in his hand. He glanced at it and read the two emojis in the message from Kostya's spiders—a pair of eyes and a car. It was a simple enough way to tell him that they had eyes on her. His concern ebbed to an acceptable level, and he returned to his work. He and Ken, the conditioning coach, discussed some changes to training plans for three of their fighters with upcoming fights as they stood at the edge of the grappling mats.

"Have you heard back from the producers yet?"

Ivan shook his head. "They said it could be as late as March before they make their decision."

"And if they ask us to be this season's camp?"

Ivan shrugged, still uncertain what he wanted to do. "I haven't decided."

"I understand." Ken and Paco were the only two around

the gym who did. They were the only ones who weren't constantly asking for updates. "You talk to Erin about hiring a couple of PTs?"

Ivan grimaced. "Shit. I forgot. I'm sorry. I'll talk to her tonight."

"No rush," Ken said with a wave of his hand. "It's just something I think would elevate our training camp. If we can offer in-house PT, we can recruit high-level talent to fight for us."

"Erin has some expansion plans she's been working on," Ivan said before stepping onto the mats to adjust Davor's forearm position and the angle of his back. When he returned to the edge of the mat, he continued, "She thinks we should bring in a nutritionist, a sports medicine specialist, and a compliance officer to handle USADA, TLDR, and all of the other licensing and regulation groups."

"That sounds like a solid plan," Ken remarked and then nudged him with his shoulder. "You need to teach me your tricks for finding a woman like that."

"Like what?"

"Smart, ambitious, gorgeous," Ken listed off. "Most of the guys here are infatuated with her. We hear those heels tapping on the gym floor and—"

"Hey!" Ivan warned, scowling at Ken who laughed and put up both hands in a sign of surrender. "Go find something constructive to do, yeah?"

Alone on the edge of the mats, Ivan watched his fighters and tried not to think about how many of the men he trained wanted to fuck his wife. He wasn't blind. He saw the stares and the open adoration of Erin. He couldn't blame them. He did the same thing. The few times any man had dared to flirt with her, he had controlled his jealousy by reminding himself that she was honest and loyal. She had chosen him, of all the men in the world, to be her man.

Certain he would forget to mention the PT question, he wrote a note and stuck it to her computer monitor. He was surprised to see that she hadn't cleared her desk as she normally did at the end of her workday. Whatever he had walked in on, whatever had caused Ruby to cry like that, had to have been terrible. It had been so jarring it had interrupted Erin's normal workflow.

He moved the mouse to put her computer to sleep, but her open email caught his attention. She sorted and emptied her inbox every single day. She was meticulous about keeping an uncluttered inbox, so seeing that many messages waiting for her reply was strange. Wanting to help if he could, he glanced at the subjects to see if he could answer any of them.

But he didn't get beyond the first email.

It had been sent less than ten minutes ago from the fertility clinic. The subject made it clear it was both of their preliminary results. He hesitated before clicking to open it. Worried that the results would upset Erin if they confirmed her fears, he decided it was better to read it first so he could deliver the information in a way that would protect her gentle heart. He couldn't bear the thought of her crying or blaming herself for being unable to make a baby with him. He meant what he had said a hundred different times. He hadn't married her for her womb. He had married her for her heart and her goodness and the way she loved him.

There were several attached lab reports, but he skipped

downloading them and read the message from the nurse instead. He didn't understand what he was reading at first. The medical terms jumped out at him. *Volume. Morphology. Motility. Total Count.*

He collapsed onto her desk chair as his shocked brain finally understood. He read the message from the nurse again and again. *Normal ejaculate volume. Poor motility. Very low sperm count. Normal morphology.*

Poor motility.

Very low.

It's me.

I'm the reason Erin can't get pregnant.

The bottom dropped out of his stomach as a reality he had never even considered washed over him like acid. He had never had problems getting hard. He had never had problems ejaculating. He had never had an STD. He was fit and healthy.

This can't be right. I'm not sterile.

He read the results again and found the attached semen analysis report. He read each line and the notes from the lab. Each result twisted like a knife to his gut. He could feel his happy life and future with Erin slipping away with every word and number on the analysis.

He returned to the email and read to the end. The doctor wanted him to repeat the analysis two more times and refer him to a dick doctor. She suspected he had suffered an injury at some point in the past that had caused his problems.

Memories of groin strikes in the heat of combat and accidental hits to the nuts during training raced through his mind. The carefree way he had laughed off those injuries, the way he had carelessly exposed himself to damage for money and pride, sickened him now. The stupid choices he had made as a younger man were robbing him of the future he wanted with his wife.

Erin.

Oh, fuck.

Erin.

Gripped in a panic, he shot to his feet. All this time she had suffered and berated herself for failing to conceive, and the whole time he was the problem. He was the reason she couldn't have a baby. He was the reason she was unhappy and brokenhearted.

She'll leave.

The thought struck him cold. Erin wanted a family more than anything. She was born to be a mother, and if he couldn't give her that, she would have every right to leave and find a better man. A whole man. A real man.

An invisible vise squeezed his chest so tightly he couldn't breathe. For a moment, he thought he might be having a heart attack. He leaned forward, both hands on her desk, and closed his eyes. He tried to slow his racing heart and breathe deeply, but his body fought him at every step—his stupid, useless body.

"Ivan?" Paco asked in a rush of concern. "*Estás bien?*"

"I…need…to…go," he spoke haltingly, each word a battle to grit out between his clenched jaw.

"Is it Erin?" Paco hurried into the office. "Did something happen to her?"

He shook his head and exhaled a shuddery breath. "No, she's fine. It's me."

Paco's face darkened with worry. "What's wrong?"

"I can't," he choked out. "I just can't."

Overwhelmed, he shut off Erin's monitor. "I'm leaving."

"Okay. Sure. We can handle it. Don't worry." Paco trailed him across the office and out into the gym. He rubbed his hand on Ivan's back in a fatherly way. "Whatever it is, you'll get through it. You always do."

"Not this time," Ivan replied with defeat. "Not this time, Paco."

After that, it was all a blur. He stumbled out to his SUV and left the parking lot. He didn't have a destination in mind. He just drove. His brain wouldn't stop taunting him with visions of Erin holding a baby that wasn't his or Erin marrying someone else, someone who looked disturbingly similar to Teague. All the times he had imagined her singing to their baby, feeding their baby and bringing their baby to the gym were replaced with images of her doing that for another man, a better man. A real man who could give her the family she deserved.

For the first time in his life, Ivan faced a problem he couldn't solve with his fists. He couldn't slay this monster. He *was* the monster.

All his greatest fears had manifested. He had always been afraid that he would ruin Erin's life. He was an ex-con, a former mafia enforcer, a prize fighter. He wasn't educated. He was covered in the evidence of his sins, tattoos that caused people to judge Erin for loving him.

And now? Now, he couldn't give her what she wanted most. If she stayed with him, she would forever wonder about the life she might have had. The life she lost by marrying him. The life he stole from her.

Even as he tried to prepare himself to lose her, his heart wasn't ready to give up. His hands tightened on the wheel, his knuckles turning white as he held on for dear life. *Please don't leave me.*

CHAPTER SIXTEEN

A S I LISTENED to a recovering mom with four young kids tell her story, I decided this was the best spontaneous decision I had made in a long time. The meetings I had attended for the loved ones of addicts were helpful, but this was a different experience altogether. It was eye-opening to hear these strangers discuss their troubles and describe their struggles to stay sober. It gave me a better understanding of what was happening inside Ruby's head.

Now that the initial shock of hearing about the sexual abuse happening inside the jail had passed, I was angry. Furious, actually. I wanted to burn that fucking place down. I wanted everyone involved to be arrested, paraded through public, shamed, and sent to prison. I wanted to shine a light on the horrible corruption and force the local government to fix it.

I needed evidence before I could do that. I needed irrefutable proof of what was happening. Would Ivan help me get it? Would he arrange a meeting with Kostya? If I got the proof, I would need a strategy. Lena would be the best person to ask for help on that account. She was scary smart and sneaky as hell and understood how to work the media for maximum impact. A media expose would probably lead to faster arrests and changes than giving the evidence to someone like Eric Santos, who, despite his best intentions, didn't have the power needed for an issue like this.

After the meeting ended, I left the meeting at Ruby's side. We skipped the refreshments table with the questionable donuts and the burnt coffee. "These meetings need better catering."

Ruby snorted. "Seriously, sis?"

"I'm just saying," I answered in a sing-song voice, "that if they had a taco bar, I would stick around to socialize."

"You're ridiculous," Ruby replied with an amused shake of her head.

"I'm starving, actually," I admitted. "I skipped lunch because of my meetings and then got distracted at the gym, and now we're here so…"

"Do you want to stop for tacos on the way back to the gym?"

"Do you?"

She rolled her eyes. "I asked first."

"Yes."

She yanked open her door and hopped into her seat. "Was that so hard?"

"Obviously," I muttered while reaching for my phone at the bottom of my purse. "I'm going to see if Ivan wants me to grab him something to eat, too."

"I watched the guy eat fifty eggs for breakfast. I'm pretty sure his answer to that question is always yes."

"Generally," I agreed with a smile. I held up my phone to unlock it with my face and noticed the dozens of messages from Benny and Lena. "Oh, my God!"

"What?"

"Vivian is in labor!" I hastily typed a message in the group chat. Seconds later, Benny replied with an update. "This is so exciting!"

"Is it?" Ruby seemed uncertain.

"Of course, it is! Babies are always exciting."

"If you say so," she replied, still unconvinced. "I need to stop by the gym or have Ivan bring home my bag. I left it in the break room."

"I'll tell him." I swiped my phone screen and tapped his number in my recent calls list. The ring tone repeated four times before going to voicemail. "Hey, it's me. We're headed back to the Warehouse. Ruby left her bag. We're going for dinner after if you want to come with us or we can do takeout for the house. Call me back. Love you."

Beside me, Ruby was on her phone. As I drove across the church parking lot, she said, "I'm making a list of all the guards I remember and the ones I think were in the room that night. Do you think Ivan knows anyone that can get into the employee records at the jail? Someone who can get copies of the work schedules? We could figure out who was working that night and make a list of potential perpetrators in that room. Then, we could see if any of them have ties to Mueller or Teague."

"He knows someone," I said, thinking of Kostya.

"Good."

I didn't tell her that there might be another angle we could work to get more help from Ivan's old crew. If Mueller and his cronies were trying to push into Houston and become bigger players in the underworld scene, Nikolai would want to stop him. If we could dig up connections between Mueller and what was happening in the jail, Nikolai could use that to run Mueller out of town.

"Where's Ivan's SUV?" Ruby asked when we pulled into the Warehouse parking lot.

"No idea." I parked in my usual spot. "He probably had to run out on an errand."

But, as I stepped inside the gym and caught Paco's attention, I realized something was very wrong. He shuffled toward me, his arthritic legs moving as fast as they could, and my stomach clenched with anxiety. I hurried to meet him and asked, "What's wrong?"

"Ivan," he said in a rush. "Something happened in the office. He was upset. He looked like he was having a heart attack. He said he had to go, and he left."

"Did he say where he was going? To the hospital?" I asked, starting to shake with fear. "Do you think it was a heart attack?"

"I don't know, Erin," Paco admitted, just as upset as me. "He looked bad. Pale, sweating, breathing hard."

"Was it a panic attack?" Ruby asked after hearing the description.

"You said he was in my office?" I prompted Paco. "Doing what?"

"He was behind your desk. He may have been reading email?"

Without another word, I raced to my office, my heels clacking as I precariously maintained my balance. Ruby jogged by me and said, "I'm going to grab my bag. I'll be right back."

In my office, I moved to the chair behind my desk and sat

down to see if anything was different or missing. I noticed a note in Ivan's terrible handwriting to ask Ken about a physical therapist. I quickly woke up my computer and found myself staring at my inbox. My gaze settled on the one read email at the very top of the inbox. It was from the fertility clinic.

My heart flipped in my chest. Was this what had sent him into a tailspin? Was it what I feared most? Was I completely infertile? Or worse? Had they found something seriously wrong with me in the ultrasounds and bloodwork?

I opened the email and quickly scanned the message from the nurse. My legs went wobbly, and I was glad I was sitting down as I reread the part about Ivan's semen analysis. *Oh, no! Oh, God!*

No wonder he panicked and left. All this time, we had assumed the problem was me. He must have been blindsided to learn he was almost sterile. He was a proud man, alpha and aggressive and protective, but under that hard exterior, he had a gentle and loving heart. He had spent so much of his life feeling unworthy and unwanted. To find out that he was the reason we weren't conceiving must have been like a knife to the chest.

And now he was out there, all alone, panicking and probably imagining the very worst. I was sure he was thinking of every catastrophic possibility. Was he afraid I would leave him? That I would want someone else if he couldn't give me children?

Surely, he remembered what he had always told me about not marrying me for my womb. I hadn't married him for his sperm. I wanted a family with him, but there were so many ways to build one. More than anything, I wanted to be with him. He was my family. He was the love of my life.

"I have to find him." I closed my inbox and shut down my computer. Hurrying out of my office, I practically ran to the back of the gym to find Ruby. She had gone to the break room to get her bag, but I didn't see her when I poked my head through the door. Her old messenger bag was still sitting on a chair, and the trash can was out of its cabinet and empty. Had she taken out the trash?

Needing her to hurry, I made my way through the back storage and supply room, skirted the edge of the utility room, and shoved the heavy rear door. "Ruby?" She didn't answer, so I stepped into the alley—and froze.

The trash bag had been ripped open, and trash fluttered around the alley. There black tire marks on the pavement, and one of Ruby's sneakers was on the ground. The evidence told me everything. She had been taken.

Overcome with rage, I stormed back into the Warehouse and stalked to the office, pushing by Ken and Paco to enter it. I headed straight to the security monitors and tapped at the keyboard until I found the feed I needed. I rewound the recording until I saw a truck leaving the alley and kept going until Ruby was just stepping out of the back door. I let it play at regular speed and watched as that son of a bitch Kavanaugh dared to kidnap my sister right there behind our gym. She tried to fight him off, but he hit her with a closed fist, right in the face, and she sagged.

"You motherfu—," I growled angrily, not finishing the word as adrenaline flooded my system. Spinning around, I strode to Ivan's desk and reached into the top drawer. I grabbed the box of staples and tore it open, sending staples

192 | ROXIE RIVERA

flying everywhere. The key I was looking for clattered onto the desk. I snatched it up and crouched down to unlock the bottom drawer. Inside, I found what I needed—the VP9SK he kept for security.

"Whoa! Whoa! Whoa!" Ken hurriedly spluttered. "What are you doing with that?"

Pistol and extra magazines in hand, I stated the obvious. "Shoot someone, if I have to."

"*Mi'ja*," Paco urged in his fatherly way, "you can't leave here with that gun."

"Actually, I can—and I am."

They both jumped out of the way as I strode out of the office, my shoulders high, and my legs surprisingly sturdy. The fear and panic from earlier had vanished. Infuriated, I was a woman on a mission. I was going to get my sister back and find my husband, and it was going to be a very bad day for anyone who got in my way.

CHAPTER SEVENTEEN

I VAN HAD BEEN driving aimlessly for at least two hours when he finally realized his phone was vibrating on the floorboard of the passenger seat. He didn't remember tossing it on the passenger seat, but he must have. How else would it have ended up on the floor?

Unable to reach it while driving, he merged into the nearest exit lane and joined the long line to get off the loop. When he was finally clear of the bumper to bumper traffic, he pulled into the closest gas station and parked. He grabbed his phone, glanced at the screen, and was taken aback by the number of missed calls and messages. It was déjà vu for the morning Erin had been attacked.

Two more messages from Ken flashed on the screen. He opened the string and read them from the newest to the oldest.

NOW.

CALL ME!

Call me!

Where the fuck are you?

IVAN ANSWER YOUR PHONE!

Do we call the cops?

What do we do?

Ruby got taken.

Ivan WTF!

PICK UP THE PHONE.

Erin took something from your desk.

Erin is in trouble.

Ivan! Call me!

He could feel the vein in his neck jumping as he reached the end of the messages. *My gun. Shit. Fuck.*

Desperate to find Erin, he called the only person who could help him right now. Kostya answered on the first ring. "Where are you? I've been trying to reach you for—"

"I know," Ivan cut in harshly. "I know, okay? Do you know where she is?"

"Ruby or your wife?"

"Both, but my wife first."

"Erin's GLS is parked outside her ex-boyfriend's house."

"Fuck." He rubbed his forehead. "She must think he has Ruby."

"He doesn't."

"You're sure?"

"Yes."

"Fuck." He squeezed the bridge of his nose. "Erin has my gun."

"Is she any good with it?"

"Fucking be serious, Kostya," Ivan snarled.

"I am."

Blowing out a noisy breath, he said, "Yes, she is actually. She has a permit. She practices at that indoor range. The pink one for women."

"Good. As long as Teague tells her what she wants to know, he'll be fine."

"And if he doesn't know what she wants to know?"

"Then, he's fucked."

"And my wife will go to prison for killing an innocent man," he shouted angrily.

"He's not innocent, and there's no way we would ever let Erin get arrested," Kostya insisted.

"The guys at the gym," he said, thinking of the texts. "They've probably already called the police."

"No, they haven't. One of my spiders took care of it. You don't need to worry about that." Kostya sounded as if he were moving around. "Listen, I just got back into town with Nikolai. I've got one of my spiders on Erin and the other on Mueller."

"What about—"

"Ruby is with Mueller," Kostya interrupted. "She was taken by Kavanaugh. We tracked him to the Cedar Port area where Mueller has a storage warehouse under one of his shell companies. I'm sending you the address. I'll meet you there. Don't go inside without me."

"Why can't I—" He grunted when Kostya hung up without any other explanation. Still worried that Erin would actually kill Teague, he called her. He collapsed back against his seat when she answered on the third ring. "Erin!"

"Ivan! Where are you? Are you okay? I know you saw the email, and you have to know—"

"Not now, *angel moy*. Not now," he said firmly. "We'll talk about it later. Are you with Teague?"

"How did you know?" She gasped and hissed, "Are you having me followed?"

"Clearly, I had reason to," he snapped back testily. "Please tell me you haven't shot him yet."

"Of course I haven't! I didn't need to," she added, her voice strained.

"What? Why not?"

"He's already dead."

CHAPTER EIGHTEEN

O F ALL THE things I had expected to find when I walked into Teague's house, this wasn't one of them. Maybe I should have considering the phone call I had with his firm. I had called his office first, thinking that he would be at work, but the receptionist has rudely informed me that he no longer worked there. It had been clear from her tone that the decision to leave the firm hadn't been Teague's.

The front door to his house had been unlocked. I don't know what compulsion made me try the handle when he didn't answer the doorbell or my insistent knocking. Maybe it was a sixth sense that something was wrong inside the house.

Everything looked normal when I stepped into the entry-way. I had called out his name a few times, but there had been no answer. Walking through his brightly lit and beautifully decorated home without his permission had felt so intrusive. I should have stopped. I should have retraced my steps and left.

But I didn't.

I kept going until I reached his home office.

And there he was.

At first, I thought he had fallen asleep in his office chair. His head was tilted back, and his eyes were closed. It was only when I noticed the splatter on the wall behind him and the strange dark spot on his suit jacket that I understood he wasn't sleeping. He was dead.

Heart hammering in my chest, I inched closer to the desk until I could see the gun on the floor by his left hand. He had shot himself in the chest, right over his heart. I didn't think it was vanity that made him spare his face. It had to have been a meaningful decision to give his mother a chance to say goodbye to him with an open casket.

Looking around the scene, it was clear he had planned this. He was freshly showered, his hair combed just so, and his face clean-shaven. His suit was properly pressed. His shoes were shined. He had his grandfather's pocket watch peeking out of his vest. The chain gleamed under the lights. Even his pocket square was perfectly pleated.

He had a note, neatly printed, and signed in front of him. I read it and started tearing up when I got to the part about his beloved bloodhound Ranger being boarded at his favorite doggy spa. Teague hadn't valued his own life enough, but he loved that dog and had made sure he wasn't here to witness the end.

I read the note again, paying attention to his reasons for ending his life. He mentioned one bad decision leading to another and that he let greed rule and ruin his life. He apologized for everyone he had hurt and warned that his full story would be told soon.

What did that mean? Had he spoken to someone? A journalist? A detective? The FBI? Was there an investigation in progress?

My phone rang and startled me. Clamping my hand over my mouth to stifle my shocked yelp, I tried to show my racing heart. I reached into my purse for my phone, gaze fixed on Teague's strangely peaceful face, and answered without looking at the screen. I had barely put the phone to my ear when I heard Ivan's voice.

"Erin!"

"Ivan! Where are you? Are you okay?" My earlier fear for his well-being trumped the fact that I was standing in the middle of a suicide scene. "I know you saw the email from the clinic, and you have to know—"

"Not now, *angel moy*. Not now," he insisted. "We'll talk about it later. Are you with Teague?"

"How did you know?" Gasping as realization dawned, I spun around, expecting a shadowy bodyguard to be standing somewhere behind me, and hissed, "Are you having me followed?"

"Clearly, I had reason to!" he exclaimed. "Please tell me you haven't shot him yet."

"Of course I haven't!" Did he really think I planned to walk in here and start popping off rounds? Looking back at Teague's body, I said, "I didn't need to."

"What? Why not?"

"He's already dead."

There was a long moment of silence before Ivan lost it. "Get out of there right now, Erin. Turn around and run."

"Will you calm down? He wasn't murdered. He killed himself."

"For fuck's sake," he said loudly. I could just imagine him wiping a hand down his face in exasperation. He grumbled something in Russian, reminding me yet again that I really needed to apply myself to the course I had purchased, and then switched back to English. "Call the police. Report the suicide."

I hadn't been expecting that advice from him. "Are you sure? Usually, you tell me not to talk to the police."

"This is different. He may have a video security system. If he doesn't, his neighbors might. You're there. It's barely getting dark. People are coming home from work. Someone has already seen you. If you run now, if you don't report it, you're going to come under suspicion." He went quiet and snarled under his breath, "*Eto piz 'dets.*"

He was right. This was fucked up.

With a tired sigh, he instructed, "Call Eric."

I was sure I had misheard him. "You want me to call Eric Santos. Eric, Vivian's cousin. Eric, the detective who hates you and who you hate right back?"

"Yes, Erin, that detective. He's an asshole, but he's honorable. He's honest. You can't trust anyone else right now. We don't know how far the corruption in the jail goes, *zvyozdochka.*"

He was right. There wasn't anyone else in the department I could trust. "Okay. I'm calling Eric right now."

"Go out to your car. Get inside. Lock the doors. Keep it running."

"I will." I glanced back at Teague. "What about Ruby? Kavanaugh took her."

"I know. I'm on my way to get her back."

"How?"

"Kostya," he said—and that was all he needed to say.

"Please be careful, Ivan."

"I will be. I'll see you as soon as possible. And, Erin, if you see anyone that looks like a threat, you fucking leave. Do you understand? You leave, and you drive to Nikolai's house. You'll be safe there."

"Oh!" I remembered suddenly. "Vivian is having the baby!"

"What? Right now? *Blyad.* You'll still be safe there even if Vivian and Nikolai are at the hospital. It will be crawling with his soldiers. When you're done with Eric, ask him to escort you to Nikolai's house. Okay?"

"Okay."

"Erin?"

"Yes?"

"I love you."

I closed my eyes and let his voice wash over me, calming me and centering me. "I love you, too."

"Hang up. Do exactly what I said."

I hung up and dug Eric's card out of my wallet. It was creased but readable. I dialed the number and walked to the front of Teague's house, stopping to peek out the curtains before I opened the door and stepped onto the porch.

"Eric Santos speaking."

"Eric? This is Erin Markovic."

"Erin." He seemed surprised to hear from me. "Are you okay? What's wrong? Are you in trouble?"

"No, I'm not in trouble." *Yet.* "I'm actually at a friend's house, and um," my throat tightened as the reality of what I was about to say hit me, "he's dead."

"Where are you? The address."

"Wait, Eric! Please, don't call anyone. Please!"

"Why not? What's going on, Erin?"

"Listen, do you remember at the hospital when you accused me of hiding the truth about the attack?"

"Yes."

"You were right," I said in a rush as I hurried out to my SUV and nervously checked each window to make sure no one was lurking inside. "I was hiding something, but it's not what you thought it was."

"What was it?"

A woman straddling a motorcycle at the end of the block interrupted my train of thought. She wore a helmet, so I couldn't see her face, but she waved at me to communicate that she was friendly. I kept my eye on her as I got into my vehicle and locked the doors. Watching her in the rearview mirror, I finally answered Eric. "The men who attacked me were trying to scare Ruby and me."

"Ruby? What the hell does she have to do with anything?"

"Something is going on inside the jail, Eric. Something really, really bad," I said and started my engine. "Rape. Murder. Sex trafficking. Ruby was one of the victims. She was in the room when some guards murdered a prisoner. An ICE prisoner," I explained. "They targeted those women because nobody would listen to them, and they were going to be deported anyway."

"Fuck!" Eric shouted. "I heard a rumor," he admitted. "More than one. About sex inside the jail. I thought it was the usual bullshit of guards trading favors for sex. I didn't think..." His voice trailed off. "The priest at my mom's church told me that undocumented workers were going missing. I looked them up, and they were all ICE holds. I assumed they were deported and left it at that." He seemed pained as he confessed, "I didn't care. They weren't guns or gangs. They were just dishwashers and maids. *Fuck.*"

"Eric, listen, you can berate yourself later, but right now, I need help."

"Where are you?" After I rattled off the address, he said, "Stay there in your car. If anyone else in a cop car shows up, you call me, and you keep your doors locked. Don't get out. Wait for me."

"Not a problem," I assured him. The woman on the motorcycle was still there. She picked up her phone and seemed to be aiming it at my vehicle. A second later, my phone dinged. I glanced down at the screen to see a message from an unknown number. I swiped to open it.

Unknown Number: *My name is Sunny. I work for Kostya.*

I sagged with relief against the seat and typed a text for her. *I'm waiting for Detective Santos.*

Sunny: *Good call. He's one of the few I trust.*

Feeling much safer with one of Kostya's associates so close, I let my thoughts turn back to Ruby and Ivan and Teague. My heart was heavy as I remembered the last time I saw Teague. Should have I known then? Should I have recognized the haunted darkness in his face as a sign that he was going to end his life?

I wasn't sure how to answer that question. I suspected nothing I could have said or done would have changed his mind. He was too far gone to help. Whatever he had done, he must have known that he was going to be killed to ensure his silence, or he was going to spend the rest of his life in prison.

Kavanaugh.

I scowled at the thought of that prick. I wasn't sure how things would shake out when Ivan went to retrieve Ruby, but if I knew Ivan, he wasn't letting Kavanaugh out of his sight until he paid dearly—and with a great deal of pain—for his crimes against my sister.

CHAPTER NINETEEN

KOSTYA BEAT IVAN to the storage facility not far from the Baytown landfill. The scent of rotting garbage was heavy in the air when he stepped out of his SUV. If it was this bad on a chilly January evening, he couldn't even imagine how disgusting it must smell during the summer.

"You'd think a real estate mogul would remember location, location, location," Kostya joked before tossing a pump shotgun at him. "It's loaded, but you might need these." He slapped a box of shells against Ivan's chest. "And this." He handed him a bulletproof vest. "It won't do much for that giant potato head of yours."

"I'm not shooting anyone." He handed back the shotgun, shells, and vest. "And neither are you."

"I'm not?" Kostya seemed surprised to hear that. "Isn't what why I'm here?"

"We are not going to shoot up Nikolai's rivals while his wife is in labor with their first son," Ivan decreed. "We're going to talk to Mueller in the way he understands best."

"Money?" Kostya asked with a scowl. Like a petulant child, he threw the weapons and vests back in the trunk. "Do you know how long it's been since I did any work?"

"Not long enough," Ivan remarked, noticing the way Kostya favored one leg over the other. "You need rehab."

Kostya sighed and rubbed his face in both hands. "Not you, too."

"What?"

"Holly. All day. She's demanding I go to rehab."

He watched the stiff way Kostya moved and said, "If you fuck like you walk, I can see why."

Kostya slapped him on the back of the head. "Fuck you."

"I doubt you can move your hips enough to even get it in," Ivan needled.

"You know, for someone who needs my help, you are a serious asshole."

Ivan grabbed Kostya's shoulder and gave it an encouraging squeeze. "Stop being a stubborn dickhead and go to physical therapy."

Kostya shrugged off his hand and slammed the trunk of his car closed. "Being a stubborn dickhead is all I've got left."

Ivan didn't doubt that at all. Holly had to love Kostya as much as Erin loved him to put up with him when he was like this. Falling into step behind him, Ivan surveyed the windowless building. It looked like every other storage facility and distribution center along the channel. Most were filled with cargo that came from the nearby port. Furniture, electronics, vehicles, clothing—if it came across the ocean on a ship, it ended up in warehouses along the bays and bayous.

"How many men are here?" Ivan had a feeling they were about to be vastly outnumbered.

"Not that many," Kostya answered and reached back to adjust the pistol tucked into the waistband of his jeans. He lifted his leather jacket to cover it. "But enough to kill us if they want."

"Let's hope they don't," Ivan groused as Kostya jerked open the door and entered the brightly lit building.

Ivan let his eyes adjust from the dusky darkness outside to the bright fluorescent light overhead. Kostya paused, letting him take the lead. He walked deeper into the warehouse, surprised by how empty it looked inside. Only a quarter of the space was filled with pallets and containers. There was no way this place was making any money at all. It had to be a front.

"Ivan!" Mueller greeted with a sickening smile. "So good of you to come! I wasn't sure you would accept the invitation."

Someday, he swore silently, *I'm going to knock that smile right off Mueller's stupid fucking face.*

"I would have come sooner if you had sent an invitation directly to me." He stopped a few feet in front of Mueller. "Where is my sister-in-law?"

Mueller whistled, and two men brought her out of a room on the right side of the building. Her face was swollen, and her nose looked broken. Seething, Ivan snarled at Mueller, "Who the fuck hit her?"

"Not me," Mueller assured him, his hands raised to show he was innocent. "I told him to take her without causing any injury, but he doesn't listen very well."

"He?"

"Kavanaugh, of course," Mueller said and indicated the man holding her by the right arm. "He's very fond of putting his hands on your sister-in-law."

Ivan's nostrils flared at the disgusting remark. "I hope he's enjoyed using those hands. When I'm done with him, he won't even be able to scratch his ass."

Mueller laughed. "You know, Kav, I think he's actually serious."

Kavanaugh, stupid as he was, grinned. "He can try."

"I won't be trying anything," Ivan promised, staring down Kavanaugh until he dropped his gaze like the soft little punk he was. Turning his attention to Mueller, he demanded, "What the hell do you want?"

"Well, what I really want, I can't have," Mueller replied cryptically. "I mean, I could have it, but I don't think my wife would appreciate that dalliance any more than you would."

As Mueller's meaning sunk in, Ivan's hands curled to fists at his side, but he kept his temper in check. Knocking his teeth down his throat wasn't going to solve anything. At least, not tonight.

"The property," Mueller said finally. "I want your property. For free," he added as if Ivan needed the clarification. "I need that land to secure the rights to develop and to get my hands on that big pile of government money."

"You did this," he gestured to Ruby's face, "over some fucking property?"

"I tried to buy it from you, but I could tell when Erin left my office that you two weren't going to sell. I would have tried to sweeten the deal to get your cooperation, but my hand was forced due to unforeseen circumstances. So—here we are."

"Teague?" he asked, wondering how Mueller knew about the man's suicide.

"Yes," Mueller said with an exaggerated sigh. "Him getting fired this morning over the firm's audit and the missing money has caused significant problems for my investors and me. The auditors will turn over their findings to the board, and the firm's board will launch an investigation that will probably catch the attention of the Feds. Just a few hops and skips and the Feds will realize that Teague tried to replace his massive loss by laundering money overseas. Africa," he said with a disgusted look on his face. "I warned him about touching those people and their money." He turned toward the corner of the warehouse and the pallets there. "And their guns."

Ivan glanced at the pallets and shipping containers. "That stupid bastard worked with arms dealers?"

Mueller shrugged. "He's book smart, not street smart. That will be a problem once he's in prison."

Ivan hid his shock at the realization that Mueller didn't know about the suicide. He thought Teague was still alive.

"Unless he talks," Ivan warned. "Negotiates a deal with the Feds."

"He knows what happens to men who snitch," Mueller replied confidently. "He'll stay loyal and do his time."

"Sounds like you have it all worked out," Ivan said, all the while wondering how angry Mueller would be when he realized he had it all wrong.

"Plan your work, work your plan," Mueller parroted smugly. "So, do we have a deal? The sister for the land?"

Ivan shook his head. "No."

Ruby whimpered with shock. She sent him a pleading stare, silently begging him to save her. Did she really think he would leave her?

"No?" Mueller echoed. "What do you want?"

"You can have those two pieces of property and three others in my portfolio."

"In exchange for?"

"Ruby."

"Obviously."

"And him." Ivan pointed at Kavanaugh.

Kavanaugh's face went slack. He whipped his attention to Mueller and seemed to finally understand he was expendable. "Sir, you can't be—"

Mueller shrugged. "Sure. Take him. He's replaceable."

"Wait! Sir! Mr. Mueller!" He let go of Ruby and tried to reach Mueller, but two of his former friends showed how little loyalty they had by blocking him.

"It was nice doing business with you, Ivan." Mueller ignored Kavanaugh's continued shouts and pleading. "I'll have my lawyers get in touch tomorrow."

Without even a glance at Kavanaugh, Mueller walked away, proving what Ivan had always known. The man was a hateful little coward.

Speaking of cowards…

Ivan stalked toward Kavanaugh who looked ready to bolt. Kostya kept him from running by lifting his weapon and warning, "I'll shoot you in the dick if you make me chase you."

With Kavanaugh under control, Ivan reached for Ruby and tugged her into a brotherly embrace. She collapsed with relief and clung to him. "For a second there, I thought you were going to let them keep me."

"I told you before," he said gruffly, "you're family."

"Jesus, you almost sound as if you actually like me," she said with a sniffle and a laugh.

"Well, you're growing on me," he admitted and awkwardly patted her back. "Like a mushroom."

"Jerk!" She punched him with her balled-up fist, but he barely felt it. "I'll have you know if I were a mushroom, I would be a white truffle, expensive and rare."

"And loved by pigs," Kostya commented.

Ruby frowned at him. "Who asked you?"

"No one," Ivan said, stepping between them before they started to argue. He turned his attention to Kavanaugh, who looked like he was about to piss his pants. "Not so fucking tough now, huh?"

"What are we going to do with him?" Kostya asked, a ravenous gleam in his eye. He had been sidelined too long and needed to get back to doing what he did best.

"Where's your closest black site?"

"About ten minutes from here."

Ivan enjoyed the petrified look on Kavanaugh's face. "Let's go."

A short time later, Ivan and Ruby stood side by side in a soundproofed garage behind an old, rusty single wide. He had bandaged her nose with supplies from Kostya's first aid kit. He would take her to see a private doctor in the morning, but he had seen enough broken noses to know when they needed surgery and when they didn't.

Silently, they admired Kostya's skill with ropes. Naked, gagged, and hanging by his bound wrists, Kavanaugh looked every bit the pasty weasel he was. The pathetic hatred he had for people who didn't look like him was on full display in the tattoos emblazoned on his skin. He had finally stopped crying, but he had a river of snot running down his face.

"So, who's first?" Kostya asked, handing him a length of pipe.

Ivan held the pipe in his hands, testing the weight of it against his palm. It was a good size, big enough to inflict damage but not so big that it would cause fatal injuries as long as they stayed away from his head and major organs. He looked down at Ruby and extended the pipe. "Ladies first."

She stared at the pipe and bit her lower lip. When she didn't take it, he gently took her wrist, turned her hand, and wrapped her fingers around it. She clasped it tightly, holding it in her shaky hand, and then looked at Kavanaugh. He could feel the anger vibrating under her skin. No doubt, she was reliving the pain and humiliation he had inflicted upon her.

Taking a step forward, she said, "Sixty-three." Her voice wavered as she repeated the number. "Sixty-three." Her arm flexed. "That's how many times you pulled me out of my cell and raped me. That's how many times you used me like I was some disposable fuck doll without feelings." She raised her arm high and asked, "You think I can swing this pipe sixty-three times before my arm gives out?"

Kavanaugh screamed into his gag, but his cries for mercy were ignored by Ruby. The first whack of the pipe against his outer thigh had Kavanaugh howling with pain. Ruby let loose a primitive growl of pain and anger and vengeance and hit him again.

And, as it turned out, she absolutely could swing that arm sixty-three times.

CHAPTER TWENTY

B Y THE TIME Ivan and Ruby finally arrived at Nikolai and Vivian's house, I had practically worn a stripe into the hardwood floors in the sitting room from pacing anxiously back and forth. Boychenko had taken custody of me from Eric and hadn't let me out of his sight since arriving at the house. He had tried to distract me, but I couldn't concentrate on anything.

As soon as I spotted them walking up the sidewalk, I raced out of the house, Boychenko close behind, and rushed out to the meet them. I reached Ruby first and grabbed her in a panicked hug. I checked her over, taking in the broken nose and the swollen hand. She was guarding her right arm, probably from an injury sustained during her kidnapping, and her clothes were different.

"I'm okay," Ruby assured me. "Really." She gestured to her face. "This is worse than it looks."

I hugged her again. "I was so afraid."

"I'm sorry."

"Don't be sorry." I squeezed her tightly. "I'm glad you're back."

"Only because of Ivan," she said, stepping back to give us some room.

His tender gaze fell on me, and he placed his big, warm hand along my face. I nuzzled into his touch and let him draw me into his arms. Like Ruby, he smelled of a strange, cheap soap and had on different clothes. I decided it was better not to ask why. Not now, at least.

"Can we go home?" I asked, desperate to feel safe in my own house, with my husband and my sister close.

Behind us, Boychenko said, "I'll drive your car home tomorrow, Erin."

I turned to thank him and saw that he had my purse and coat in his hands. "You're a sweetheart," I told him, lifting up on tiptoes to give him a quick peck on the cheek. "Thank you."

He glanced away and cleared his throat. "You're welcome."

Ivan's hand settled onto the small of my back. He nodded at Boychenko and escorted Ruby and me to his idling SUV. We drove home in silence, none of us ready to talk about what had transpired today. Ivan held my hand, keeping us connected, and glanced over at me every now and then to smile. In the backseat, Ruby seemed oddly serene. Something had happened while they were gone, something that helped her find some peace.

When we finally made it home, we trudged inside, all three of us completely sapped of energy after our long, trying day. Ruby hugged me one more time and squeezed Ivan's arm before telling us good night and climbing the stairs to her room. Alone in the kitchen with my husband, I stared at him, trying to decide what to ask him first. I chose to start with the safest possible question. "What did Mueller want in exchange for Ruby? That's why he took her, isn't it? To get leverage over you?"

"He thinks he's a fucking genius," Ivan snarled. "He thinks he got one over on us, trading Ruby for the property, but he didn't even know Teague was dead."

"I don't think Teague went quietly into the night." I put my hand on Ivan's chest and relished the hard strength of him under my fingertips. "I think he put something into motion that Mueller won't be able to stop."

"Good." Ivan dipped his head and sought my mouth. I melted into his embrace and his seeking kiss, gripping his shirt in both hands and refusing to let him go. He must have sensed I was still upset about him leaving the gym like that. He touched his forehead to mine. "I'm sorry I ran like a coward."

"Oh, Ivan," I said in a rush and kissed him again. "I'm so, so sorry you found out like that." Tears stung my eyes, and I tried to blink them away, but imagining his pain at that moment broke me. "I'm so sorry."

"Please don't cry," he begged, his voice thick. "Please, Erin," he said roughly. "I can't handle it when you cry."

"I'm sorry. I'm just overwhelmed."

"No, it's fine. I'm an asshole. You can cry. You can even hit me if it makes you feel better." He shuddered and then weakly pleaded, "Please don't leave me."

"What?" I reared back in shock. His face was a mask of pain so deep that it hurt me to see it. "Ivan!" I cupped his face and forced him to look at me. "I'm not going anywhere."

"I understand if you—"

I kissed him, interrupting whatever terrible thing he was about to say. "I'm Not." I kissed him again. "Going." Another kiss. "Anywhere." Another kiss. "Without you."

"But you want a baby—"

"Yes, I do, and we'll have one someday," I promised him. "Maybe not the old-fashioned way. Maybe not a baby that grows in my belly. But we will be parents. We'll have a family. Together." I stroked his face and prayed he would understand how deeply I loved him. "Ivan, you are more important to me than anything in this world. You. Just as you are."

"I love you so much, Erin," he said in a rush of emotion. "I never thought I could feel like this. I never thought I could be this happy." He crashed his mouth to mine, his hands tangling in my hair as he lost control to passion. "All I ever wanted was to make you happy. To give you everything in life that you want."

"And you have," I assured him. "You have, Ivan." I turned my face and kissed his palm. "You are all I need to be happy. Just you."

We shared a deep and loving kiss. It was a moment I would remember for the rest of my life. Just the two of us, in our kitchen, making a promise to love each other no matter what. It was a tender moment that filled me with so much hope for our future. It wasn't going to be easy. There were probably going to be more tears and sadness, but I wasn't afraid of tears or sadness.

As long as we were together, we could face anything.

CHAPTER TWENTY-ONE

Nine Weeks Later

"SCOOT OVER," IVAN urged as he shuffled from our master bathroom back to the bed. He was bent slightly at the waist and grimaced with discomfort when he finally made it to the bed and had to climb onto it.

"I told you this bed was too tall."

He rolled his eyes at me. "Yeah. Yeah. Yeah."

"Do you need help getting comfortable? I can move some pillows for you."

"No! You stay right there. Flat with your legs up, remember?"

Now I was the one rolling my eyes. "Dr. T said to do this for fifteen minutes after the procedure! Not for an entire day!"

"I don't want to risk it," Ivan replied and then gestured to the front of his shorts. "I'm out of order for at least a month. If this doesn't work, you'll have to wait until I'm back in fighting shape."

That morning, I had held Ivan's hand before he was wheeled into surgery. His specialist had diagnosed a serious varicocele and strongly suspected surgery would improve the health and number of his sperm. Ivan had agreed immediately to the procedure, and we were both hoping it would have a positive effect.

After he was discharged from his outpatient procedure, he sat beside me and held my hand as we had our first IUI. He had been giving samples at the clinic for the last ten days to get enough of his swimmers for an insemination procedure. It was a complicated process of collecting, washing, and choosing the strongest sperm to inject directly into my uterus. I had taken a course of injectable drugs to prepare my body for the baby bomb. They had made me a hormonal mess, but it was worth it for a better chance to conceive.

"Okay," Ruby announced as she entered the room with a basket. "I've got one ice pack, three scoops of strawberry ice cream, a phone charger, a Gatorade, and a Cherry Coke. Did I forget anything?"

"Nope!" I happily took the bowl of ice cream and the Coke. Ivan took the other things and got himself situated, lifting up the sheet and gingerly placing the ice pack on his family jewels. "Thank you."

Ruby made a face. "Yeah, I'm going to bleach my brain now. If you two need anything else *not* related to his swollen speed bag, message me."

Ivan made a throaty sound of irritation. "I hope she remembers this the next time she needs help."

"I'm pretty sure she's doing everything she can to *never* remember the sight of you putting an ice bag on your—"

"Yeah," he cut me off with a frown. "I get it."

Deciding it wasn't nice to tease him, I leaned over and kissed his cheek. "I love you."

He harrumphed and let out a noisy sigh. "I love you, too, even if you are enjoying my predicament a little too much."

"I mean, listen, if this works," I gestured to my belly, "I'm going to be in a world of hurt in nine months when your giant-headed baby is born."

He seemed to consider that. "Okay. That's fair, I guess."

"I think so." I rubbed his arm. "I know this whole experience has been difficult. Going to therapy at the clinic, letting that doctor fondle you with his cold, wrinkly hands, and choosing to go through with this surgery today. I know it wasn't easy, and I know you're in pain."

"It's worth it," he assured me. "I'd do it all over again."

"Well, let's hope you don't need to go through this again." I turned my gaze back to the television where the nightly news was beginning. The last few weeks had been wall-to-wall coverage of corruption, the rise of white nationalism in the city, and the sex trafficking ring operating inside the jail. Five guards had been arrested and indicted for the murder of Maria del Carmen Riojas. Kavanaugh, who had been dumped in front of an emergency room with multiple broken bones and two severely fractured hands, was in jail awaiting trial for his attacks on my sister and a dozen other former prisoners who had come forward.

"He did a good thing, you know?" Ivan gestured to the television. "Teague," he clarified, as if I didn't know. I raised an eyebrow at that, wondering how many pain pills he had taken. Before I could ask, he said, "Do you think he knew? That sending you that box of files and hard drives would lead to this?"

The morning after Ruby's ordeal and Teague's suicide, the three of us had been having breakfast when the doorbell rang.

I had expected to find the police or Detective Santos waiting on our doorstep to ask questions, but it was just a box addressed to me from Teague. He had mailed it the morning he before killed himself. There was only a short two-word note from him inside.

I'm sorry.

His apology made more sense once I realized that he had been the distributor for the films made inside the jail. He had been the one who took requests and handled all of the money from the operation, money that went back to the hate group Mueller controlled. There weren't any direct links to Mueller, of course. He was too smart for that and used shell companies and pass-throughs, but there were enough dots to connect to make it very clear that he was involved.

It hadn't taken Ruby or me long to decide what to do with all of the information inside. We contacted Lena, who gave us the names of journalists and social justice influencers she trusted to handle the story correctly. Ruby had insisted on making copies to send out to the journalists and influencers. We put the originals and our own set of documents in two different safes, just in case.

It hadn't taken long for the first story to break. Once it hit the papers and the internet, all hell broke loose. There were protests, mass resignations, and public shaming unlike anything I had ever seen. Mueller had lost his right to develop that area along the proposed I-45 expansion. Yuri and a group of local Houston developers and contractors he had hand-picked put together a lightning fast bid that won the right to the project. Our land was tied up in the deal because of Ivan's trade with Mueller, but working with Yuri was a much more acceptable and highly profitable situation.

"I think Teague hoped it would," I answered finally. "I think he trusted me to do the right thing."

"Like you always do," Ivan said, lifting my hand to kiss the back of it. His gaze drifted back to the television. "Can we watch something else?"

"Like?"

"Something not so serious," he said, wincing as he shifted. A thought seemed to strike him because he smiled. "*Beauty and the Beast*! Let's watch that."

"What? Why?"

He yawned and wiggled his toes, further confirming my suspicion that he was high as a kite on pain meds. "Ruby says I eat eggs like one of the guys in the movie."

I busted out laughing. "Oh, my God! You do! You're Gaston!"

"Well, let's see," he gestured to the television.

"Okay." I found the film in our Disney+ app and hit play. As it started, I snuggled closer to Ivan and ate my ice cream. When I was done, I put my head on his chest. He began to comb his fingers through my hair in the most gentle way. There was something so wonderful about these happy, quiet moments of marriage.

Not that those quiet moments ever lasted long in this house.

"*Blyad*," he exclaimed as LeFou and Gaston sang about wrestling and biting and danced through the tavern. "I fucking am Gaston."

Overcome with the giggles, I buried my face against his thick, muscled arm. He might have the boisterous manners and the oversized diet of Gaston, but his big, loving heart was all Beast.

And it was all mine.

The End.

Also by Roxie Rivera

Her Russian Protector
Ivan
Dimitri
Yuri
Nikolai
Sergei
Sergei 2
Nikolai 2
Kostya
Alexei

Fighting Connollys
In Kelly's Corner
In Jack's Arms
In Finn's Heart

Debt Collection
Collateral
Collateral 2

About the Author

A *New York Times* and *USA Today* bestselling author, I like to write super sexy romances and scorching hot erotica. I live in Texas on five acres with my husband, two daughters and our wild and ever-expanding menagerie of pets.

You can find me online at www.roxierivera.com.